OUT OF TOWN

Stories About Those
Other People

JOHN HEUSSLER

BALBOA.PRESS
A DIVISION OF HAY HOUSE

Balboa Press books may be ordered through booksellers or by contacting:

Balboa Press
A Division of Hay House
1663 Liberty Drive
Bloomington, IN 47403
www.balboapress.com.au
AU TFN: 1 800 844 925 (Toll Free inside Australia)
AU Local: 0283 107 086 (+61 2 8310 7086 from outside Australia)

Because of the dynamic nature of the Internet, any web addresses or links contained in this book may have changed since publication and may no longer be valid. The views expressed in this work are solely those of the author and do not necessarily reflect the views of the publisher, and the publisher hereby disclaims any responsibility for them.

The author of this book does not dispense medical advice or prescribe the use of any technique as a form of treatment for physical, emotional, or medical problems without the advice of a physician, either directly or indirectly. The intent of the author is only to offer information of a general nature to help you in your quest for emotional and spiritual well-being. In the event you use any of the information in this book for yourself, which is your constitutional right, the author and the publisher assume no responsibility for your actions.

Any people depicted in stock imagery provided by Getty Images are models, and such images are being used for illustrative purposes only.
Certain stock imagery © Getty Images.

Print information available on the last page.

ISBN: 978-1-5043-2208-9 (sc)
ISBN: 978-1-5043-2210-2 (e)

Balboa Press rev. date: 08/05/2020

CONTENTS

PROLOGUE

The bush moulded the character of the Australian pioneers and the children who came after them. It bred people with initiative who took responsibility for their actions and their own well-being. The rules for survival were determined by the natural conditions imposed by the land and not by bureaucrats in a distant city. The lawmakers were too far away to help and too remote to be much of a nuisance, so people relied on themselves and their friends. They did their own thing, which was not always acceptable in the eyes of their more conventional cousins. They faced their difficulties or found ways around them. Those who didn't found themselves at the bottom of the heap.

Many left the land seeking relief from the droughts and failing markets, or because there were too many children to inherit the farm. They adapted to the needs of a closer community, but they were always subtly different. Others sought jobs working for those who succeeded in handling the system.

These stories are not about the landed gentry or the classical picture of the stockman. They are about those who make up the endless variety of bush people, their strengths and their failures, and in many cases what happens when they interact with their city cousins.

WAITING

She was waiting with her children in the lounge at the little country airport. While quietly sobbing, she nursed a baby. As I entered, a young boy of about two, pushing his stroller onto chairs on a mission of general destruction, stopped short and ran to clutch her skirts. I hesitated in the doorway before closing it against the freezing wind. I had seen a car parked outside, but I still hadn't expected to find anyone in the small waiting room on such an inhospitable night. Nonplussed, I furled my dripping umbrella and dropped my swag on the nearest bench. It was so cold, and now the rain had started to come in over the hills, propelled by a gusty wind. *Bugger, I wonder what she's doing here?* I thought, hesitating.

Satisfied by a large steak at the local diner, I carried a comfortable bedroll and was keen to use it. With its coffee machine, carpeted floor, and mandatory toilets, the terminal had seemed a good place to camp while I waited for my friend to arrive early next morning. We had arranged to fly back to Sydney at first light. Hence, my initial reaction wasn't altogether charitable.

"Hello," I said, somewhat mollified as I observed her obvious distress. "What brings you out on a night like this? I'm Ted Bancroft. Hope I'm not intruding." *Looks like I won't be able to roll out my swag after all.*

Startled and frightened, she looked up at me. She tucked away a breast and defensively shifted the baby. Fear and red blotches from previous tears could not hide the beauty of her soft face and the depths of her hazel eyes. While wearing faded jeans and a sweater under an old topcoat for the cold, she wasn't really a candidate for a fashion magazine, but I am sure she could have been if she had tried. I endeavoured to put her at ease.

"I can always go somewhere else if you wish," I offered. "I would much prefer to wait in a corner here if you can put up with the company. Why don't I boil up the coffee machine and make us a cup? I could do with one, and you look as if you could use it."

Relaxing a little, she gave me a tentative smile. "I'm Kate Blanchard. Macy is the demon here, and this is little Susie." She held up the baby for a burp. "And yes, I would love a cup of coffee. Anyway, I can't chase you outside on a night like this.

"I am afraid we are all a little stressed," she added. "My sister-in-law had an accident today, and my husband, Jim, is flying in from Wilcannia tonight to see her. I'm so worried about him in this weather."

I had often flown light aircraft on emergency dashes, and as I filled up the coffee maker, my thoughts went out to the man in the little machine up there in the clouds somewhere to the west. A bloody fool to attempt a flight in these conditions. He wouldn't help his sister or the rest of the family if he wrote himself off, but I understood his compulsion to try. The pressure front had developed more quickly than most of us had anticipated, and a clear afternoon had rapidly deteriorated. Now, rain lashed the tarmac outside. I was grateful that we had delayed my own flight till next morning.

I imagined him, with the charts on the seat beside him, hurtling through space in an aluminium box at 180 knots. Eerie green needles, steady on black backgrounds, replaced his normal senses of up, down, or right way up. Thoughts would be racing through his head like a train through a tunnel.

Weather seems to be closing in. Go to full instruments. Better get a revised terminal forecast from air radio. Getting near the mountains; check lowest safe altitude. Request permission to climb two thousand feet. Rougher up here; review procedures for blind approach to the airfield. Set altimeter for pressures at terminal. Careful—might be inaccurate out here; change frequencies. Check airfield altitude. Should I continue? Been good under the hood; need practice. OK so far. Pick up that wing.

The workload would sap his ability to make quick logical decisions, forcing errors from his inexperience. No airliner this, with a co-pilot to navigate and an autopilot to control the machine while it followed a radio beam into a commercial airport. This was stress, more stress, and critical judgements crowding in on each other like sheep jostling through a counting gate.

We listened to the rain drumming on the tin roof and a bit of thunder in the distance. Even Macy was becoming subdued. I made a couple of paper aeroplanes for him out of old flight plans lying on the floor to distract him. Kate attempted to quieten the baby with some more food. Macy tired of the game and chewed the ends off the planes. Back to Mum. At least he wasn't attacking the furniture with the stroller. A gust of wind threw a giant handful of rain at the plate glass front of the shelter. I wondered whether Kate realised the situation up in the sky. "What happened to your sister-in-law?" I asked. *Best keep her talking.*

"The usual country accident. The cows got through the fence into the oats, so I asked Jim's young sister, Lucy, to come over and help me get them out. She loves riding and often helps us on the farm. Her horse fell trying to wheel a calf through the gate. The doctors say she has concussion and a fractured vertebra in her neck. We are all very worried about possible spinal damage. I feel so dreadfully guilty because I asked her to help. Her family is with her, so I've come out to meet Jim. We all told him not to come. We can't do anything. It is up to the medicos now, but they are pretty iffy out here. We'll get her to Sydney as soon as she can travel." Kate was in control of herself, but only just, and she accepted another coffee with a shaking hand. "Do you think Jim could possibly land in this? I wish he wouldn't try. He'd fly into Hades for Lucy. He's so pig-headed, and he doesn't trust the medical services. They used to be great, but the whole structure out here has gone downhill since the wool crash."

I thought, *And the only navigational aid is an old, non-directional beacon—no electronic landing system. One day we might have that satellite navigation the Yanks talked about. The NDB approach is really only safe for a cloud base of a thousand feet with these hills around.* I didn't tell Kate that, but I sure worried about it. *Time I rang air radio and ask them to warn him of conditions here,* I decided. I asked Kate if that was OK.

"Yes, please—oh, please do," she said.

There were usually phones at the terminals for pilots to report arrivals and submit flight plans, but this one was useless. The receiver was on its cradle, but I found the cord had been cut and used to tie the door shut. *Wish I had driven into town and rung them before.*

"When is he due?" I asked Kate.

"He should have been here by now." She looked at her watch. "It will take fifteen minutes to get into town." Then the runway lights came on, switched remotely from the aircraft.

We heard his plane come across the field—a steady drone above the noise of the rain. It passed over the beacon and departed on the required heading to the north. A set time on that leg, a ninety-degree turn, and hold for fifty-two seconds, then another turn onto a new heading towards the south. That should put him on final approach for runway 18. The turns and timing of the legs in such an approach have to be precise. Hard enough with help, but almost impossible on your own in a high wind and turbulent air. Seemed hours before we heard him returning. In spite of the cold, I was sweating now.

Again, I was with him in the cockpit.

Turn onto base leg; watch the time interval. Slow down the machine, more flap. Check wheels down. Still no visual. Turn on to final. Did I allow enough for the wind drift? How much wind? Doubts crowding in like fruit bats to a mango tree. *Five hundred feet. Check speed; should see runway lights. Three hundred feet; that's the limit. No lights, no visible reference—get the hell out of here. Full power, stick back, half flaps, wheels up.*

His landing lights cut through the rain. They picked out the distorted faces of the horrified little group behind the plate glass of the lounge like some giant flashbulb. He would only have seen the wet roof as it slid under his nose. The terminal building, not the runway under his belly, and most of the three hundred feet had evaporated. The crescendo of the engine at full throttle rattled the windows and shook down another bucket of rain. We ducked our heads inside the room like soldiers avoiding an artillery shell. I looked down. My hands gripped the window rail, knuckles white as if I held the controls.

I turned to Kate as the sound of the motor receded. No red in her face now. Trembling with fright, she was pale as the snow on the hills above the airfield. I held her and her baby, Macy clinging to our legs. Would he try again? Had he planned an alternate airfield? Did he have the fuel to reach it? Did he climb out on a course that avoided the mountains to the east? So many questions.

I joined him again.

Get back onto safe climb out path. What is the departure heading? Dump flap. Too soon, you fool. Acceleration makes it feel nose-up; don't forward stick. Settle climb speed, wings level. Why does the bloody ball not centre? Watch direction gyro. Have to compute time and course to alternate. Hands shaking—that bloody terminal was close. Turbulence off the mountain; yawing to starboard, keep her level. Bugger—dropped the pencil. Still in cloud. Why are the needles dancing? Doesn't feel right. Believe the instruments—remember, got to believe the instruments. Wings level. Panic. Fear. Discipline collapsing under pressure. Vertigo. Icing now. Carby heat, quick …

Silence except for the drum of the rain on the roof and the howl of the wind. A great bottomless well of silence as we waited. No sound of an engine. He wasn't coming back here. Was he heading elsewhere? Tension mounted, and I suffered with her. We had to contact the air radio. We had to know.

I frantically drove them into town and found a phone. I rang my friend David, whom I knew in Civil Aviation. No news. Give it an hour before we worry the family. We booked a room in a motel with a phone, and one next door for me. We put the children to bed and waited … and waited … Worry and fear grew inside us like a cancer, eating our guts and swelling within us until we couldn't contain it. We prayed. We told the family, and they prayed too. They came and waited with us in a strange motel room for news that would change our lives.

We rang air radio again.

"We've lost contact with him," they said. "We will ring you a soon as we know anything. Don't leave this phone."

I couldn't help imagining the worst. *Right rudder, level the wings, Pull out of the dive, full power. Good, no icing now, but I must be close to the hills.* Then the final agonising reality. *It's clearing, I can see—trees, nothing but bloody trees. Pick two big ones …*

I wondered whether he would have had time to adjust his direction. Did he remember, in that instant of terror, the flying instructor saying, "If there is no way out, pick two big trees and go between them. That way, you wipe the wings off and the fuel with them. The impact in the cabin will also be reduced."

The phone rang, its loud jingle making us all jump. "We have reports of an aircraft crashing into the hills to the south of the airport," said David, now manning the air radio. "It is near a homestead, so the owners of the house are investigating. We will advise you as soon as we know anything. We have ordered an ambulance and the fire brigade. Please stay near the phone."

"Don't give up hope, Kate," I said. "People have survived difficult landings before." But she was at breaking point, and Suzie was crying for a feed. I felt for her as if I had known her for years. I made another cup of coffee for us all.

The call came at two o'clock in the morning. This time, David was much more relaxed. "Tell them it is OK," he said. "The plane is a mess, but Jim survived. He hit two trees with his wings, and the cockpit ended up twenty feet away. He is injured and concussed, but the paramedics from the ambulance reckon he will survive."

Kate collapsed. Great racking sobs that she had held in all night escaped. But she could still ask to be taken to the hospital immediately to meet the ambulance. Their reunion would be a joyful affair.

11

I drove out to the airport to meet the plane from Sydney. I thought that if ever I had a girl like Kate, I would not risk losing her because of a stupid desire to be there at any cost.

DREAMTIME CALLING

Jimmy Eagan, Deputy Shire Clerk, Mundamba Council.
On completing his first day, Jimmy closed the office
door and pretended not to admire the new brass name
plate. He felt as if he had finally arrived after all the
training over the last few years. He had a new job back in
his old town, but he knew none of the local people now,
so he felt the loneliness a newcomer would encounter.
He would have to organise his spare time.

He enjoyed his football and was a competent player,
so he reckoned he would walk down to the club and see if
there was a place on the training squad. It would be a let-
down from work and perhaps a way to find new friends.

Jimmy was born in a tin humpy down by the river.
He remembered his aboriginal mother and his alcoholic
father, a camel driver of European origin. Returns from
extended trips with the animals were unannounced. The

13

door would fly open. *Where are you? You fat bitch. Get that piccaninny of yours to find me a beer.* He hid terrified behind his mother, waiting for the inevitable bashings, and then he went to the fridge. No ice cream in there, mainly beer, and not much tucker either. Everyone knew when the camel driver was in town by the bruises on his family. When Jimmy's arm was broken and his concussed mother was unable to defend him, Social Security took action, sending him to a foster home.

Mr. and Mrs. Eagan, his foster parents, gave him love and stability. Later, they gave him education, a work ethic, and even their name. Jimmy had heard of other kids sent to less caring families. Knowing how lucky he was, he returned their affection but in secret grieved for his mother. Because his white genes had dominated, he could pass for a swarthy immigrant, making his path through school and early employment somewhat easier. Jimmy grasped his opportunities, even accepting the current posting in his home town. He would face his memories and make it home.

Needing more power in the centres, the football team snapped him up. Bit of a find, really; he combined well with their half back, a nimble aborigine they called

Slippery. Together, the two ran through the opposition like water down a drain, passing and sidestepping at will. Jimmy wouldn't go past the local team because he had resolved to make a career in local government. He was proud of what he had achieved and did not intend to stop now. He wanted to show the Eagans that their confidence in him was justified.

One evening after training, he gave Slippery a lift home.

"Thanks, Jimmy," Slippery said as he got out of the car in front of the old house he shared with numerous relatives. "What ya doin' on Sundee?"

"Nothing much," replied Jimmy. The flat was clean and the garden watered.

"The Mullarammy people are having a get-together out at the five mile, Sundee arvo. Our elder, old Charlie Hawks, is off the grog now and getting old. He reckons if he doesn't tell us young fellers some of the old stories, they'll be lost forever."

"Aw, I don't know." Jimmy hesitated. "I got to be careful not to take sides now I'm working for the council, whatever the rights and wrongs. Mustn't get into any land rights arguments or protests"

"Bugger the protest—that's another matter," retorted Slippery. "This is learning about the old days. Hear your mother came from down the river, so you ought to come out. There'll be no booze."

"OK, I'll give you a lift out," promised Jimmy.

Jimmy worried about Sunday afternoon. He was very comfortable in the contemporary society he had adopted, but still there was something dragging him back to his heritage. The intensity of his reaction to the evening at the five-mile water hole surprised him. They sat round a fire, cooking an odd snag and boiling the billy, while old Charlie Hawks rambled on about the dreamtime and the legendary birth of the plains. The tales went on into the night. No alcohol spoiled this session. They had learned that lesson the hard way.

Ancient stories told in the heart of the timeless land, with the glow of the full moon reflecting on the water, wove a spell over the little group—the survivors of a tribe overtaken by changes that were inevitable in a developing world. No longer a recipe for a lifestyle but a fable or a religion, the dreamtime bound them together and relaxed them into a togetherness not experienced in the beery mists of previous parties.

The following weekend, a few of them met with Charlie to discuss that afternoon. He knew of a bora ground about forty miles west of town. Why not try to resurrect some of the dances that told the stories of the creation? Why not try to regenerate the old culture lost in time? The way of life was gone forever, and Jimmy didn't want to go back to sleeping on the stones and eating goanna when and if he could catch one, but he *was* searching for identity. The dances were OK, but he would draw the line at any of those initiation ceremonies. He had looked up what *bora* meant! He reckoned that those still in the no man's land between the cultures might gain some comfort from a better knowledge of their roots as long as they didn't expect to live like the old people in a modern world.

So the date was set: the Saturday night closest to the next full moon. As the ground was on a pastoral holding, the owner would be reluctant to allow the exercise for fear of the area becoming a sacred site or being subjected to land claims. Knowing him, several amongst the group pointed out that the place was already registered, and after repeated assurances, they received his blessing. They had to camp, but the warm nights of summer removed the need for much shelter. Pray for no rain and a cloudless evening. No one had organised a corroboree before, so old Charlie was the boss. Jimmy hired a minibus, and some took their cars. They'd assembled about thirty souls in all, plus the kids. Jimmy was pleased they wouldn't do the secret dances forbidden to women and children this time, and at least that ruled out initiation.

Charlie led the long march into the bora ground from where they had to leave their cars. They found it on a mesa: an ancient plateau standing solitary and gaunt amidst the endless rolling plains. The barren surface, dry and rocky, yielded little growth except for the stunted mulga trees, dark and sticky and pointing at the sky. In a place where even they did not grow, the little group traced strange patterns, curves, and lines of stones so carefully placed by ancient hands. Between the lines were flattened pads where one imagined the feet of long past generations telling stories, still related in the dream time myths. All the soil had washed down to build the plains, but the remaining rock stood for ages in testimony to forgotten people and their tales.

It was such a culture shock for Jimmy to discard clothing and replace it with yellow ochre and white bands in strange patterns. He felt like a chook without feathers. What did the patterns mean? Charlie had some answers, but many were lost in antiquity. Then there were hours spent while he tried to explain the steps and the meaning of the complex ballet of the plains. Miming the hunt for the great kangaroo, the birth of the mountains, and the course of the rivers, they told the stories in dance and movement. All afternoon they prepared under the guidance of their elder. Unfortunately, his memory was limited, but they got the general idea, and a bit of impromptu embellishment seemed acceptable. They rested a while at sunset and unpacked their meals—not traditional fare, but that was not the point this evening. After all, they were still living in the twenty-first century. They lit the fire and watched the moon rise blood red in the east.

The barrenness and dryness seen under the blazing sun of a hot afternoon gave way to silvery mysticism under the stars. What a magic place it was in the full light of the moon, especially with their painted bodies moving and swaying, and the weird sounds of the didgeridoo stirring the silence of the night. Jimmy danced the strut of the old emu and found he *was* the old emu. He was becoming part of the land and the animals it supported. Feelings and ideas flooded his brain. He hopped and squatted and rolled and jumped to the beat; his being was one with the creatures and people. It was unlike anything he had ever experienced in the rocking night clubs of the city. So much meaning, so much contact with the land, and so much understanding brought new emotions previously buried deep in his aboriginal past. The white man in him stood back, looking on in amazement. He had found his roots.

But they were only half his inheritance. The other half was in a far-off land under a cloudy sky, dressed in fur against the cold. Hard to reconcile that. He was grateful to the Eagans for the Western culture and the preparation for the realities of modern life, but his glimpse of the spirit of the dreamtime had shattered the certainty of his adopted Anglo-Saxon traditions.

AN OLD OAK TABLE

I found it in the chook house when Uncle Allen died in 1976. Hens roosted on its edge, and laying boxes obscured its surface. It wasn't the top that caught my attention; that was covered with more guano than Nauru Island. But the stump of a broken leg hung off a corner and a carved motif, still visible through the grime, and it shouted at me, demanding rescue.

I had a photograph of that table taken in the days of its youth and beauty. Larger then, with its extension leaves in, it stood solid and serene like the people who sat round it. Its carved legs proudly displayed the family crest cunningly worked into intricate patterns at each corner. The silver setting, gleaming in the candlelight, reflected its gracious curves in the soft, smooth polish of the oak surface.

Maids in starched aprons and white caps stood behind the chairs, and the butler prepared a turkey for presentation at the sideboard while my great grandfather presided over the proceedings with that inflexible, unyielding discipline that governed his own life and those around him. No sloppiness was permissible. The men sat straight in their dinner suits with shirts like cardboard, and they deferred to decisions from the head of the table. The little girl in the foreground had obviously been brought down to say good night and would soon be banished to the nursery. The ladies, their bulky long skirts hidden amongst the delicately shaped legs of the table and their bodices dripping with lace, compressed their bosoms to display delicate cleavages. Eyes downcast, they concurred with the statements of their menfolk. They would air their own opinions later in the privacy of the drawing room, leaving their spouses to pass the port unchallenged.

I cherish that photograph, all brown and posed, taken on a glass plate with "1888" etched on the back. It not only brought to life a bygone age of chivalry and authority but is also one of the few contacts I have with the legendary ancestor who had brought our name to

Australia. With the death of his grandson, my Uncle Allen, I became the sole survivor of the family and the beneficiary of his will. Not that it amounted to much.

I had come to inspect my inheritance, but the whole estate seemed to consist only of a small farm, a few cows, and a yard full of hens, not to mention the debt at the bank. I planned to sell the lot, but not before I had a better look at the old table in the chook house.

Uncle Allen was the elder brother of my deceased father, and there was a delicious mystery about great grandfather's family, so I had searched in vain for some family records. Years ago, careful questioning of both my father and grandfather had yielded tight lips and a firm refusal to discuss the matter, but my mother had later relented and told me all she knew.

It appears my great-grandfather, Sir Cedric Houndslough, was an efficient and quite ruthless merchant in the young colony of New South Wales. Seeking a less competitive environment than Victorian England, he had emigrated to the new colony and prospered, selling initially rum and picks and shovels to gold miners and later anything that would return a profit to the good citizens of Sydney town. He effectively used his wealth to purchase position and power until he was recognised as a respected gentleman of the establishment. Such eminence required suitable accommodation, so he built a grand house. Appropriate furniture was brought out from England, including the oak table, specially made with the family crests emblazoned on its legs. With it came a wife, and he set about establishing a family to rule.

What splendid evenings must have been enjoyed round that beautifully carved table. The rich and the powerful, the beautiful and the useful—all the worthy citizens of the city graced its boards. The children, safe upstairs in the nursery, were granted a glimpse of the finery when they came down for their fleeting visit to that other world of the grown-ups. What plans were made? What deals were negotiated over the port after the ladies withdrew to their coffee? The children were not always excluded. On Tuesdays and Thursdays, they ate dinner with the family. I imagine the stilted conversations.

"What did you learn at school today, Son?" said my great-grandfather.

"We started on the works of Virgil, Father, and I am receiving good marks for my Bookkeeping." Frederick, his only son, a clever lad, knew how to please his father. He studied the questions that might bring favourable comment from his usually taciturn parent. This paid off in trips to the city and presents that were likely to arrive out of the blue.

In contrast, a comment like, "I came first in arithmetic," from his sister would usually draw an acid, "Be quiet. Little girls should be seen but not heard."

Sophia wasn't his natural sister. Sir Cedric had reluctantly agreed to adopt his wife's niece after her father's death and her mother's subsequent nervous breakdown. Not happy with the arrangement or the revelation that his wife could bear no more children, he ignored the girl most of the time and scolded her when that was not possible. For her part, Sophia was a defiant child and rebelled against the injustice, a behaviour that led her into constant and sometimes painful conflict with her adopted father. Mealtimes with the family often ended with Sophia being sent to her room or sometimes being made to sit under the table. There, she was out of sight and out of mind behind the folds of a big white tablecloth that was used when the children were dining with the family. Sir Cedric was then able to concentrate his attentions on Frederick, his son and heir.

My mother suspected that the table became a refuge for the unhappy child. A large cover was left on when not in use to protect it from the NSW summers, so the space beneath was private and secure. It wasn't as if there was much alternative. School was a privilege for girls, and when not so occupied, Sophia was expected to learn to sew or play the piano. Visits to the garden to run or to the stables to talk to the horses were strictly rationed and ceased altogether when, at the age of fourteen, she was seen holding hands with the stable boy, Billy Turner. For Billy, immediate dismissal resulted from their indiscretion, and Sir Cedric promptly forgot his existence. Subsequent research by my mother revealed that he had obtained a position as a gardener's assistant at the school for a short while, so it is possible that Sophia maintained some contact with him. The servants winked as they discussed Billy's motives, but Sophia found in him the only person who would listen to her troubles and was interested in her chatter. Besides, helping him in the stables was fun.

Then, on Tuesday, May 13, 1893, Sophia was sent to bed early for arguing with her father. She subsequently disappeared. She simply wasn't there in the morning. Such a panic, such recriminations, such frantic imagining. The police were called in, the gardeners searched the grounds, my great-grandmother had an attack of the vapours, and Sir Cedric fumed about the house, blaming his wife for letting that ungrateful little biddy to enter under his roof.

"What would one expect of a family with no background?" he asked, livid with rage, towering over his shivering wife and, ignoring the fact that she came from the same family as he did.

They found the little boat that was normally kept in its shed at the bottom of the garden. It had sunk not far from the jetty on the other side of the river. A board in the bottom was broken with Sophia's shoe jammed in the crack. They never found Sophia, though they rowed up and down the river for ages, dragging a big frame that brought up every imaginable kind of rubbish. After tipping it in little piles on the bank, they painstakingly sorted through the trash looking for anything that may have belonged to Sophia. Not even a hair of her head was found. She had never been taught to swim and would have been unlikely to get far in her long skirts.

The coroner brought down a verdict of "death by misadventure," and the family closed ranks. Was it guilt, or was it simply ignoring the unpalatable? Whatever the reason, Sir Cedric gave orders that Sophia was never to be mentioned again by family or staff. Her existence was expunged from the family memories.

But the servants talked, and Sophia's disappearance became a favourite topic of conversation in the taverns and bars of Sydney town. Some said she had been seen on a train headed for the western plains on the railway over the Blue Mountains, and others had seen her on a ship bound for Brisbane, but proof was always lacking. The locals claimed her ghost could be seen on the thirteenth of the month rowing across the river around midnight. Such a sad end for an unhappy child.

I longed to know what happened that night and whether there was any possibility of her surviving. I felt I knew her well from that old photograph. Frederick was obviously part of the party, but Sophia stood beside him in her dressing gown and plaits, a pretty but sad little face, lost amidst the formality and finery of the dinner party. Her wide eyes and soft lips told of a beauty to come, and her image followed me through the days. Had she lived, she would have been nearly a hundred years old when I found the table. Perhaps she languished in some nursing home, pain-racked and lonely, thinking of the family who had let her down. She may have grandchildren my age. Perhaps I was not the last of the family; even if old Sir Cedric wouldn't own her, she was adopted and a blood relative of my great-grandmother.

My quest for Sophia was not new. I had tackled the telephone book, ringing hundreds of puzzled Turners, explaining my mission, and suffering either their fury or their condolences. I had even gone to Denver to the Mormon database. I had advertised in newspapers and on radio. I found nothing. Perhaps she did perish in the river that night. Or perhaps she eloped with Billy Turner. Sir Cedrick would not even have thought of that. Then I looked through the old newspapers for our own name, Houndslough—not so common, that one. I must find her if she still used it. But no, there was no response, not the faintest whisper of a lead.

The death of Uncle Allen had offered some hope. I searched the boxes under his dressing table. I searched his office, if an old desk in the corner with piles of bills stacked on pins could be called an office. I searched in the garage where he once kept his old Ford car. All I got from that were the extension leaves from the table nailed on the wall for shelves. I called his solicitor, asking about safe deposit records. Unfortunately, Uncle Allen had nothing worthy of a safe deposit. Sir Cedric's son, Fredrick, had disposed of most of the Houndslough fortune on questionable business deals, fast cars, and faster women. Uncle Allen used what was left for his daily whisky ration.

I came away empty-handed—except for the old oak table strapped down on the back of my light truck. The agents could sort the rest and dump what they couldn't sell. Hopefully, that and the farm itself would cover the debt.

Six months passed before I attempted to renovate the old table. I cleaned off the chook poo, the dust, and the egg yolk for a start. I took a sample of wood from the broken leg and eventually found some matching timber to fashion a new one. I soaked the joints and disassembled the whole structure. The top surface would have to be stripped, the joints rerouted, and the whole lot sanded down. I examined the bearers closely, testing their strength and looking for damage. Only then did I notice the pencil scribble on the vertical inside surfaces. I hastily rubbed off the last of the grime and took the boards to a good light. I stared transfixed at Sophia's secrets. Most obvious was the traditional heart shape, transfixed by Cupid's arrow heavily scored. Underneath in childish writing was, "Sophia loves Billy."

Poor little girl, with a crush on an older boy, I thought, deciphering the fainter sentences mixed up along the board.

There was more, so much more. The tormented recordings of an unloved child caught in a false morality, confined by the customs and expectations of a society she could not understand. Her adopted parents were preoccupied with their own lives, and her presence was both a nuisance and an embarrassment to them. She craved the attention of the one person who had listened to her. Over it all, her developing sexuality was driving her into the unknown. She must escape.

"Billy loves me."

"Billy is so kind to the horses."

"I like helping Billy."

"Billy kissed me behind the feed bins. I nearly swooned I was so naughty."

"Daddy caught Billy holding my hand. He sacked Billy."

"I hate Daddy."

"I saw Billy at school."

"Billy and I are going to elope."

"Billy has arranged it all. Midnight at the old jetty."

"We are going to Queensland."

"We will be Mr. and Mrs. Fairfax."

"Billy says I look sixteen."

"I love Billy."

Some of it had faded with time, but eventually I deciphered the whole sad story, written in an unformed hand in so few words. I had found my records. I had my clue. I wondered whether Sir Cedric had ever found the little diary and whether he realised the injustice he had inflicted on her. Would he feel remorse or sorrow, or would he simply preserve his own skin? Would he be enraged at the fact that her confession was written directly under his dinner plate, but he could not see it? Somehow, I couldn't imagine the old man on his hands and knees under the table, and the servants would have been reluctant to tell him even if they had discovered her scribbling.

I booked a flight for Brisbane. Best start with the nursing homes. People live longer these days, and there might be records even if she had died in the last few years. Besides, Fairfax was a lot less common than Turner.

I found her at the ninth establishment I contacted, an old home run by the Salvation Army for the poor. Bright blue eyes sparkled in the tired, old face as she sat in her chair all rugged up against the cold. Her voice quivered, but her spirit shone through, strong and challenging.

"At last," she croaked. "Wondered if you would ever find me."

"You should have called on us," I said guiltily.

"I've followed the family all these years. I have press cuttings of all your academic achievements. Pity that Frederick blew all the money and old Allen was a bum from the start."

"I've looked for you for so long," I said, kissing the papery skin on her cheek. "I think I was half in love with the image of a little girl in an old photograph. I wondered what sort of life you could have achieved in those days without money or family support."

"Oh, we had no money," she admitted, "but I chose well in my youthful infatuation. Billy was kind and true. We loved each other very much, and we got through the good times and the bad. I'd never have made a great lady."

I didn't hear her granddaughter come in. I looked up and saw a copy of the girl in the picture beside the old oak table. But this one was grown up.

IN WHOSE NAME?

Bill Mason paused in his wheelchair opposite the flats that rose sheer above the street. Encrusted with balconies like the icing on a giant wedding cake, the structure looked over the sea of fibrolite roofs jostling around it as if to keep out the distant ocean. Bill always stopped there on his way home from the shop. He stopped to remember the girl from Bosnia and to get his fix of maudlin self-pity. He would have to start painting again. He knew his landscapes were quite good, and that had provided an escape from torment before when he was forced to leave the west. He could do that. One day ... But right now, everything was too raw, too painful, the whole bloody episode.

It had all started with a flaming cat. That stupid cat and the foreign sheila who had moved into the dilapidated little cottage that had stood where the brick façade now soared skyward. Dragana was her name, but he didn't know it then. Bill had been doing a survey for his real estate firm; big, strong, sandy-haired Bill from Urandangi, with his bush drawl and city clothes. Bill's employers were looking at the possibility of a developer buying up a few of the tired old shacks to build a block of flats. That was how he had come to enter the small garden and find her looking up at the lump of enraged fur on top of the light pole.

Yowling its head off and under constant attack from a squadron of mickey birds, the cat was too petrified to work out how to get down. One glance up the pole was enough for Bill to assess the situation with the cat, but its owner was another matter.

She stood there in a flimsy wrap, obviously just out of the shower. Her wide cheekbones and blue eyes were framed by a mass of soft hair not yet contained after washing and spilling round her shoulders. Slim and tall, she gazed up at her pet, trying to give it the courage to come down from the pole. Upon becoming aware of his presence and obvious interest, she clutched the wrap more firmly around her and smiled through her embarrassment.

"Please excuse me. I come outside feeling sorry for my cat," she explained. "I know the feeling to be isolated and attacked. Is not nice. Could you please help me get her down?"

Who could refuse a request from such an attractive stranger? Besides, Bill was intrigued by her accent and the hint of past terror in her little speech. One didn't see many like her where he came from, so he was happy to help.

"Have you got a ladder?" he asked.

"There's one in the back shed," she said. "But I don't think it is very good."

Bill didn't think it was much good either, but the pole wasn't very high, so he asked her to hold the bottom while he climbed to the rescue. Of course, on the way down, the bloody cat clawed the tripe out of him. The ladder wobbled and creaked before giving way to his frantic gyrations. He landed on top of Dragana, on top of that beautiful body. The moggie cleared out, leaving them sitting there and examining themselves for injuries. They covered their confusion with unnecessary apologies and then dissolved into fits of laughter at the situation.

"When things go wrong, I think Australians have a cup of tea," Dragana suggested. He went inside and accepted the drink along with a couple of Band-Aids.

"Tell me how you came to be living here with a cat," Bill said, curious to know why she was living alone in this uninviting area.

"I come out here from Sarajevo as a refugee," she said. "I lost my home and all my family in the insurrection, so I flee from war and religious intolerance. There was nothing to keep me there."

"What do you do for a living?" asked Bill. Most of the refugees he knew were on the dole.

"I work at what you call a checkout chick at the local supermarket," she said. "I have a medical degree from Bosnia, but I am not allowed to practice here until I can pass the necessary Australian examinations."

Bill knew he was only getting a small part of the story, but it was time to go, so he rose to say goodbye.

"You haven't asked me my religion," she said as she escorted him to the front door. "Thank you for that, and for rescuing my cat."

"Don't mention it," he replied. "Couldn't care less about your religion, but I was interested in your story. Makes a man feel he gets it easy out here. Give me a bell if you need a hand anytime."

Bill knew that offering to help strangers off the cuff would get him into trouble one day, but she seemed like she might need a bit of assistance. He went on his way remembering that once upon a time, his parents, if ever so politely, would have been careful to ask about her religion. Bill held strong beliefs but couldn't understand why all those priests and mullahs and rabbis got so paranoid about it and started trying to convert their mates. "Live and let live" was a fair enough philosophy for him. He was much more concerned for Dragana's welfare, and he admired the courage required to start again in a new culture amongst strange people and without the support of family or friends. He resolved to keep an eye on her and be available if necessary.

Bill lived on his own too. At the moment, he occupied a flat near the sea, where he could see whether the surf was up enough for him to catch a wave or two in the early mornings. He had been married, and the divorce had been messy, but now it was great to get away from the bloody woman telling him what he should do all the time. Freedom, escape—it had all felt real good for a while, and he enjoyed a beer or two at the club after a long day at work. He started playing a bit of golf too, and his handicap came down as he relaxed, but he still found it was lonely coming home to an empty house at night.

Bill got Dragana a nice flat not far from the beach when the developer bought the old shack from her landlord. It was a big improvement on the cottage but she had no garden. The cat missed it, but she didn't because she spent every spare minute studying for her medical exams. The language made it a bit hard for her, so she failed a couple of times and had to wait another six months before trying again. Bill popped in occasionally to help her with her rental arrangements and the odd form that she couldn't understand. He found someone to coach her in English. He tried to do more, but she was an independent little person and wouldn't accept anything that looked like charity. She eventually relaxed a little, and they started to go out for the odd dinner. Bill gradually lost interest in the local sheilas who were indicating availability now that he was single.

"Not going to mess up in my new country," Dragana said in answer to invitations he shouldn't have extended. Not that he made many. She was so vulnerable, and he was falling for her quiet courage and gentle determination. Like a rare work of art, she was there to be treasured. It was a bit out of character, but he played the gentleman and went home to dream.

One day, Dragana rang him, her voice full of excitement and her joy flowing down the phone wires. "I've passed the examination!," she cried. "I can practice in Australia. I can do what I've always wanted to do. I can make myself useful at last."

"Good on you," said Bill. "I'll volunteer to be a patient, if you want one."

They went out on the town to celebrate. They came home and celebrated some more. With eyes misty in the glorious languor of dinner washed down with the best wine and the ocean shimmering under its moon outside, she came to him.

"Thank you for rescuing my cat," she murmured. "That silly cat and that silly ladder. I fell in love with you that day. I didn't dare tell you in case you went away. I desperately needed someone to love, someone I could rely on. I depended so much on your encouragement."

"I didn't do a great deal. You were too bloody proud," said Bill, a bit embarrassed at these revelations, "I used to lie awake at night wondering how I could make it a bit easier. But I'll accept any credit going."

He was unprepared for the surge of emotion that swept over him with her kisses. He had been kissed before, but this lifted him to another plain of tenderness and caring. He unwrapped that beautiful foreigner in front of the murmuring surf, vowing to look after her forever.

After their passion was spent, they lay in the big bed with her soft curves nestled into his body while she told him more of the conflict in her homeland and the decimation of her family in Bosnia. She knew he tried to understand, but the nightmares were still so vivid to her, and she realised he couldn't imagine the suffering and the traumas that had been inflicted on that little community.

He gently changed the subject and told her of the big mobs of cattle that roamed the dry plains out west. He told her of the dust and the flies and the thirst of the droughts and of the emerald-green grass and the wildflowers after the rains, when the rivers flooded out over the flats. Eventually they slept, and she felt safer in his arms than she had felt in a lifetime.

They woke with the sun in their eyes as it rose above the ocean, its warmth streaming in to where they lay under a thin sheet. They reviewed the promises given in the soft glow of evening love as they explored again their emotions and their bodies in the bright light of the new day. They found them true and began to plan their lives together.

"I want you to understand me," Dragana said. "So much has happened in my homeland. My youth is there. So much cruelty and destruction, so much hatred and love tore us apart. Never forget that where hatred is, love also survives. Before you commit your life to this little foreigner, I want you to come and see what made me."

"Bloody waste of time," said Bill. "I know what I've got, and it suits me just fine whatever made it."

She raised herself on her elbow and turned her clear blue eyes to the mole on the side of his nose. "We won't spend our life in bed, and even here, marriage will have hard bits. To support each other, we must understand. My background is so different from yours. Please come with me. I am told it is safe now," she pleaded.

They left for Sarajevo a month later.

What a harrowing first day as they walked the streets of the old town.

"I've never been in a city where they have to have a mob of blokes in blue berets to keep the population from murdering each other," said Bill. "Never been in a town where you are likely to get knocked down because you are a different religion from those living in that neighbourhood. I've never seen streets of houses blown to bits, with weeds growing in the ruins."

There were a few places in Sydney or Brisbane where he had to be a bit careful at night, but here he walked around all day looking over his shoulder. Not that the locals weren't hospitable. They received a real welcome from all her friends and relations, and everyone seemed relaxed enough as they filled up their glasses with vodka. The people in the shops smiled a welcome as they made their little purchases.

But when they said that they were going to see the ruins of her family's old house, her friends advised them not to go.

"That's over the bridge," they said. "We never cross the river. You'd better tell the police because there have been cases of people getting hurt over there. Besides, it is in the past, and you will revive old devils."

They went anyway. They gazed at the rubble that was a home—not one that Bill would have paid a lot for on the Sunshine Coast, but then he realised they were a bit spoiled back home. The crumbling stone walls had contained rooms that would have been comfortable enough in a somewhat crowded neighbourhood but left scant space for the sort of amenities he was used to. She explained how they had found the bodies of her mother and sister but had never found out what had happened to her father. She told of the shells and the smell of gunpowder and death. She told of rape and cruelty and hunger. She told of begging for putrid water and the stomach pains that followed. She told of flight and loneliness and refugee camps. But she also remembered to tell Bill of the kindness and support of friends.

Bill had seen the war on television. He had reckoned he knew it all. But while standing there, comforting the one he loved who had lost so much, the stark reality swam into focus: the terror, the fear, the loss, the hopeless inadequacy, and the inability to influence the madness collapsing around her.

He knew now why he had to come, had to help her exorcise the nightmares that must have possessed her and that would no doubt return with other crises that were inevitable in a lifetime. If he was to be of any use to her, he must know, must try to understand. They crept back to their lodgings, and he held her tight that night till she slept.

"You have seen the sadness and horror that drove me away," she said the next morning. "Now, let me show you the beauty and serenity that sit beside the terror and give joy to my dreams. Then we will leave, and I am yours forever."

"I don't know that I can handle much more of what we had yesterday," said Bill. "Have they really stopped shooting each other out there?"

They checked before they went. Her friends reported that the countryside was more peaceful than the city, although fierce fighting had raged through the hills during the troubles and the debris of war still lay about the countryside.

After hiring a small car, Dragana drove him up into the mountains, up over the passes, and down to an alpine lake. No snow fell in the middle of summer, but the air was crisp and clear, and the signs of past conflict were fading as vegetation grew and tracks disappeared under meadow grass.

"When we were children, my father used to bring us up here fishing," explained Dragana.

A midday sun shining on the little beach of pebbles beside the lake warmed them enough to entice them to swim, if briefly. They laid out a rug and ate a lunch provided by her friends. They talked of the opportunities they would find back home, of children and houses, of pleasures and sadness. They planned their careers, but most of all they talked of their lives together. They took pleasure as their bodies merged and their minds blended with them. They discussed all the things that people in love dream and imagine. They slept and swam again.

She sat drying in the lowering sun, the last drops of water glistening on her as she looked out over the lake. Bill took his sketchbook along the shore a little to record the scene. He planned to paint it later and already had the title: *Serenity.* Perhaps it would remind them of the beauty that remained unextinguished in a troubled country. He drew the picture in his mind.

Hugged by forest round its edge, the lake lay placid and smooth, reflecting back the sky. The rugged mountains, crowned rosy by the sinking sun, ringed it all around, standing ancient guard over peace and blessed solitude. The little noises that make the countryside buzzed about them. The hum of wasps, the plop of fish fracturing the mirror of the lake, the rustle of the leaves from a pretended breeze—all combined to make a silent sound. Amidst it all, Dragana shone, ever growing in her beauty through the meeting of their hearts and minds. And Bill? Tenderness and love expanded within him as he tried to capture the splendour all around them.

She rose and came towards him, glorious in her nakedness. He stood, the sketch already showing promise to rival nature's own magnificence.

Bill saw the mine beneath the pebbles, and her foot descending on it. His warning shout was shattered by the burst. The world stood still. An eon passed. He felt the shrapnel take his legs. He saw his love explode. Those lovely limbs all wrenched apart. And all their hopes destroyed. He saw it all and suffered years in the time it took to fall. Years compressed to moments while thinking of their loss. Was it greed or creed or race that made men plant that evil thing? What life remained? So much they had planned to do. So much they had planned to love—a perfect being shattered, broken, no more to love or play or sing.

Oh, gods! Why must your stupid captains send their men to murder in your names? Moslem, Christian, Jew look up to you. You stand for love, but war and hate is perpetrated by your troops. In whose name was this bloody deed conceived? And if indeed you all be one, I'll ask before the pearly gates, "Why must it be forever so?"

They got him back. Back alive without his legs. Back home to emptiness, pain, recrimination. What else was left to dream? Bill had brought the tattered sketch today. He'd found it crumpled in a pocket with his passport. He shook his greying head and heaved, his shoulders square.

"I'll paint the bloody scene. I'll do it now. I have to make her beauty live. I have to show they cannot win."

He swung his chair around and turned for home, past the "vacant" sign that hung where once a cat had sat.

AN OLD QUEENSLANDER

Poor old bugger. You'd think his family would look after him or put him in a home. The Meals on Wheels driver sighed and shook his head. He always found old Tom sitting in the same ancient wicker chair, teetering on the rotting floorboards of the veranda. Man and house resisted change—ignoring the placard on the partially completed building next door that pleaded through the scaffolding for tenants to "Move in by Christmas 1990."

Tom O'Grady fondled an ancient glass jar in his gnarled hands as he leaned back and gazed vacantly across the street. His bony frame was encased in a pair of moleskin riding britches that had seen better days and a checked flannelette shirt that was never properly tucked in. Wisps of fine grey hair strayed beneath a faded beanie that had obviously been knitted with loving care many moons ago. No spectacles assisted the watery blue eyes, which were too clouded with cataract to have been useful anyway. He'd have been tall once, but age had shrunk his body, and his legs were bowed from years wrapped round a horse.

He sat surrounded by his bottles, with his favourite ones stacked on the cane table beside him. Bottles were strewn across the floor and crowded out other rubbish in every corner. Bottles coloured by the fierce light of the outback, pale green ones, dirty blue ones, bottles telling of ancient remedies, bottles with marble stoppers. They threatened to spill through the gaps in the wrought-iron balcony of the old Queenslander. Some lay in boxes, and some rolled around on the bare boards. Collected from the outback rubbish heaps and stock routes or desert camps, they all had a story to tell.

The Meals on Wheels volunteer parked in front of the little house. It crouched behind its diminutive garden, dwarfed and contained by the bare brick walls of the three-storey flats that crowded the rest of the precinct. The gate had long since collapsed, and the small plot had succumbed to weeds, but even these remained defiant, the only green things in sight. To the volunteer's surprise, the creaky front door opened to his first knock. A frazzled lady in a housecoat faced him with a vacuum cleaner ready in the background.

"Hello! I'm Jim from Meals on Wheels," he said. "I'm glad to see someone here. We all worry about old Tom. He shouldn't be sitting out there in the cold."

"I'm his niece, Cathy Blaine," she explained. "I worry about him too. He'll be ninety-five next year. I'm grateful to you people for looking after him. Look, the kettle's boiled, so why don't you come in for a cup of tea? Maybe you can give me some ideas. I'm at my wit's end. We live over the other side of town, and he refuses to move."

Jim smiled. "Sure. I've finished my round. I'd like to think we could do something for the old fellow. I feel so sorry for him just sitting there."

"Jim has brought your dinner, Tom," Cathy called as he mounted the rickety stairs with the meal containers. "Come and eat it before it gets cold."

"Just leave it inside the door," came a quavering voice from the veranda. "Not hungry yet."

Cathy shrugged as she put the meal in the oven. "I come over as often as I can to clean up. We've tried to move him into a home or even to our house, but he won't leave his bottles and won't have anyone else in here in case they break the damned things. At least he's used to his own company."

"What's with the bottles?" asked Jim.

"They all have a tag inside telling where they were found, and some also record a history of some fascinating parts of the outback," she explained. "Tom has his favourites connected with his life in the bush, but most were collected by his late wife. There's the little opium bottle from the Chinese garden he visited near Winton, and the one embossed *Ellimen's Royal Embrocation for Horses* found at one of the Cobb and Co. coaching stops. He reckons another is a sauce bottle he threw away at a drover's camp on the Diamantina back in the twenties. A little medicine jar brought him and his wife together— quite a romantic tale, really."

"I'd like to hear it," said Jim, settling in to a cup of tea and a slice of the cake he had brought over for Tom.

"Why not?" she agreed, taking a rug out for the old fellow.

According to Cathy, before the First World War, Tom jackarooed on one of the big sheep stations straddling the old Cobb and Co. coach road in western Queensland. Not yet twenty and city bred, he was regarded as a bit thick at school, so his family reckoned he'd never make good in town and sent him out to the bush, where they thought it wouldn't matter. They called in a few favours, and one of their friends secured the lad a job on his brother's property west of Longreach. Tom's horsemanship was no match for the rest of the crew, and he could never think of the right reply to their jibes in time to be effective. Besides, no one bothered to explain how things worked out there, so he quite regularly made a fool of himself before he discovered his errors. Being a new chum and a bit slow to catch on, he became the butt of so many practical jokes, and he eventually ignored most of what he was told.

He therefore discounted the tales of Stirrup Iron Ned. As the proprietor of the 80 Mile Pub, a sly grog shop and coaching stop of some notoriety, Ned held a fearsome reputation amongst the jackaroos from the nearby stations, and his powerful frame grew bigger with every telling of his exploits. He regarded the land around his pub as his reserve to run the spell horses for the coaches, as well as a few sheep of doubtful origin, needed to provide mutton for the table. Any attempt by the rightful owners to run their stock on the disputed land was repelled by Ned at full gallop, swinging his stirrup iron round his head at the extremity of its leathers or wielding his stock whip with deadly accuracy. The sight of Ned astride his great chestnut horse coming full tilt at the intruder, with his felt hat glued to his head, his dark eyes blazing above his ginger beard, and his strong arm wielding the dreaded whip, was enough to send the bravest jackaroo scurrying for home.

"The boss said we have to muster that mob in the five mile paddock and take them over to the hole near the pub," said the overseer as the hands were saddling up at the horse yards after an early breakfast one morning.

"Bloody hell. What about Stirrup Iron Ned?" asked the head stockman.

The consternation spread to the ringers, who all caught their swiftest mounts, tightening the girth strap an extra notch before they set off. The jackaroos shut up. One couldn't let on one was scared in front of the men, so they relieved the tension by teasing Tom.

They dutifully mustered the sheep from the blackened pastures nearer the station and drove the mob north towards the disputed territory. They strung the animals down to the waterhole near the pub when they arrived in the late afternoon, and they sent Tom up to steady the lead while they chivvied the tail along, ready for a speedy exit.

Stirrup Iron Ned came at them like a whirlwind out of a bush fire before they reached the clay pan along the creek. Ringers and jackaroos alike fled homewards down the channels beside the coach road, leaving the flock to the mercy of the intruder who seemed more intent on venting his anger on the horsemen than diverting the sheep from his waterhole.

Tom had scored the slowest horse and had started off later than the others, so he was the first to receive Ned's attentions. He was a flat gallop over the broken ground near the creek, the fearsome whip cracking inches behind him, and neither he nor his horse saw the log in the long grass. Over they went in a flurry of hooves and legs, their momentum hurling him against more sticks and stumps. The horse got up while his attacker pursued the others, but Tom lay there without moving.

Upon noticing the problem behind him, Ned pulled up. "Go back and look after your mate, ya mob o' dingoes," he yelled as he abandoned the chase, and after a quick look at Tom, he headed back to the pub.

The mustering party relaxed as they saw Ned retreating, but the head stockman led them back to look for Tom. They found him where he fell. They were twenty-five miles from home, and the new jackaroo was out cold with a broken leg. The only option appeared to be to seek help from the retreating enemy.

"Bugger left him for dead," growled one of the party.

No one volunteered to ride to the pub and face the formidable incumbent, so the head stockman set off, accepting the responsibility of leadership.

He was met by Stirrup Iron Ned cantering back followed by one of the new Napier motor cars. Bigger and brighter than the more common Model T Fords, the

Napier was becoming a favourite of the more wealthy land owners in the North West. The big machine bucked and bounced over the Mitchell grass tussocks, blowing smoke from its exhaust and flapping its black canvas hood like a tent in a thunder storm.

The coach wasn't due till next afternoon, but the Napier's owner was resting overnight at the pub while returning from the city with his wife and Dorothy, a young nurse on her way to the Cloncurry hospital. Ned suggested they take the wounded jackaroo to the doctor in Winton next morning.

Tom woke to find two concerned females bending over him while the men fashioned rough bush splints for his leg. They emerged out of mists and receded into dreams, but Dorothy's presence took some of the pain out of his leg. The ointment they rubbed on his wounds helped too, and when they finished the jar, they threw it into the hollow of a nearby stump.

He needed all the comfort he could get for the trip to Winton next morning. The coach road was windy and rough. They lurched through the gullies on corduroy crossings and vibrated over the gidgee gibber plains until he had to clamp his teeth on a towel to prevent his screams. Dorothy used all her training to alleviate his suffering, and he responded to her kindness. Her arm around his shoulders lessened the ferocity of the bumps in the road, and her quiet support gave him the courage he needed. The trip left a lasting impression on the two young people, but by the time they passed him over to the doctor in Winton, all he could do was mutter his thanks through a pink haze of pain. She left without even knowing his surname.

The leg healed, albeit crooked and a little shorter than the other. Tom returned to work.

"We'll put you on as a ringer," said the manager. "Can't have a bloody gammy-legged jackaroo on this place."

"You can dig us another dunny pit," ordered the overseer.

Tom stuck it for a while, his original shyness returning and the last of his self-confidence departing. He drifted to other stations and other jobs, always being allocated the lowliest tasks. He helped drive the big, wild herds of Territory bullocks down to the fattening pastures of the Channel Country, but he was always the butt of the jokes round the campfire. Eventually, he settled for a boundary rider's job.

While camped in a tin hut of tiny proportions beside a waterhole, ten miles from the homestead of a remote station down the Thompson River, he savoured the isolation and retreated into fantasy whenever the demands of his job allowed. His friends were his dogs, his chooks, and the creatures that came to drink at the waterhole. He knew them by name and watched over them, tending them when sick and protecting their young. Unpainted and bare under the fierce western sun, the hut was home, and he stayed there year after year.

His employers eventually bought him an old utility so that he could drive in and help out at the station when needed. They even ran out a single-wire telephone line so that they could talk to him. Technology had arrived in the bush, but Tom used it sparingly, although he did read the old newspapers they sent out with his stores once a week.

"Why don't you take a holiday in town?" asked the boss. "Must get sick of yourself out there on your own."

"No point going in to get a skin full of grog," he replied. "There's nothing else to do there. And who's going to look after my dogs?

"Come to think of it though," he added, "wouldn't mind taking a drive up the stock route and looking around some of me old stamping grounds. Would you mind if I took the ute?"

The dilapidated utility became a common sight parked at the camps and dumps along the stock route on weekends. He carted the rubbish of yesteryear back to be stacked beside the tin hut in case it should be useful; amongst it were the old bottles that intrigued him with their colours and embossing. That was how he came to notice the advertisement in the personal column of Queensland Country Life.

Dorothy also collected old bottles. An excellent nurse, she became matron of a small country hospital, marrying the local stock and station agent and raising a family. There was not much time for a hobby between her nursing duties and her children, but the children soon grew up. Dorothy became interested in the history of the area, and she began collecting memorabilia. Her imminent retirement and the death of her husband in the Second World War left her more opportunities to pursue her leisure activities, so her collection became her passion. Glass, tinted from the hot sun of the West, fascinated her, and she found the bottles to be a great record of past events. She travelled the roads and byways in search of them, vigorously researching the history attached to each one and recording it on slips of paper.

When she visited what remained of Stirrup Iron Ned's domain, she discovered the pub had burned down in the 1920s. All that remained were some rotting stumps and a picked-over rubbish heap. After finding only a Champions Vinegar bottle and one embossed "Worcestershire Sauce," Dorothy was about to leave when she remembered the little jar of Faulding's Eucalyptus Ointment she had cast into the hollow of a stump all those years ago. As she had so often done before, Dorothy wondered what had happened to the boy they had driven to Winton in such pain. She still vividly remembered Stirrup Iron Ned's attack on the station musterers and the subsequent dash to the rescue in the old car.

She set off to retrace the path they had taken. The country looked different now because there was more grass, and thousands of small coolabah trees, seedlings from the big floods of the 1950s, had grown on the flats beside the channels. The creek beds were the same, though, and she eventually found the bend where Tom had fallen. From there, she soon located the remains of the old stump, and in it, covered by the debris of the years, was the small container.

This time she acted. As soon as she returned home, she rang the local newspaper reporter for the *Queensland Country Life*. The advertisement she placed read as follows.

Bottle Found in Stump

Would the young jackaroo injured near the 80 Mile Pub in 1914 please contact Dorothy, the nurse who helped take him to Winton? Please reply Dorothy, C/- P.O. Townsville.

It was not much, but it was enough to elicit a response from Tom, who happened to read that page wrapped around a corned brisket sandwich while on dinner camp near a bore. On countless lonely nights in the tin hut, he had remembered the trip in the Napier and the nurse who had comforted him, but he had never summoned the nerve to seek her out. His reply started a series of letters ending in a contract to meet in Townsville.

"I've changed me mind, boss," Tom told his employer. "I reckon I will take a holiday. Think I'll go and have a look at Townsville." He disappeared on the first train going north after alternative arrangements could be found for the tin hut. His dogs were a problem, but he took his favourite with him and charged the new man to look after the others on pain of eternal damnation.

Their reunion was awkward and restrained as he limped off the train at Townsville station, and shyness kept their soaring emotions bottled up inside them. She took him back to the lodgings where she was boarding and talked the landlady into providing a separate room for Tom at the back. They ate their dinner as they listened to the chatter of the other guests.

But that evening, they sat on the veranda in big, flat squatters' chairs, gazing at the moon as it lit a golden path over Cleveland Bay towards Magnetic Island. Words came to them then, slowly at first and then in a torrent—words held back for years, words that he had not even allowed to exist as thoughts in his lonely life, and words that she had not allowed to interfere with her other commitments. They found ways to express emotions that they never knew they had.

"Reckon I didn't realise I was so lonely," admitted Tom as they kissed tentatively before retiring to their beds. "Never knew what it was like to talk to someone who had common interests and was happy to be with me."

"I know," she replied. "I was okay while I had the family, but being a widow eats away at your foundations, and I always wondered what had become of you."

After a few more evenings on the veranda, they pooled their resources, bought the little house in a back street, and installed their bottle collections. She died eight years ago, and Tom retreated again into his memories.

"What are you two talking about?" asked Tom, hobbling into the room still clutching his bottle. "Reckon I'll have me dinner now."

"We're working out what we can do to make your life more comfortable," explained Cathy. "You can't just sit out there forever on your own in the cold."

"I'm not cold when Dorothy's with me," he said defiantly. "She's there whenever I'm handling the bottles. I was alone for so long. Don't take her away from me now."

Jim shrugged. He had been left on his own for ten years now, and many well-meaning people had offered help that he didn't need. "Perhaps a cherished fantasy is better than a lonely reality even if it is uncomfortable. Don't think I can help you, Cathy. See you for lunch tomorrow, Tom." He rose to go.

TWENTY-ONE GRAMS
OF THOUGHT

Jim Dougherty lay in his hospital bed dreaming, seeing again the accident as it happened. He remembered it in minute detail and flung out his arm to protect Deborah in the passenger seat, knocking over the vase of flowers on the bedside table. He saw the oncoming vehicle rearing up and displaying its ugly black belly as it mounted the median strip, before it came crashing down on his little coupe. He noticed the muffler tied up with wire and the wet patch where oil was leaking from the flywheel housing—megapixels of detail absorbed in that instant of terror. He screamed, disturbing the other occupants of the ward and bringing the redheaded nurse to his side.

Big Jim Dougherty was tough. One had to give him that. Maybe it had something to do with his childhood in the corrugated iron homestead in the scrubs of Cape York Peninsula. The cattle station was impossibly remote, so his only childhood contacts were the aboriginal kids who lived with their stockman parents in the quarters down by the waterhole below the stockyards. He and his mates were enrolled in the School of the Air, but the radio was often broken down, and his mother had little interest in supervising them. The house contained no books, so they spent their time chasing goannas or tracking dingoes through forest. What they lacked in formal education, they made up in bushcraft and the resourceful independence that came from living and surviving in a hostile environment. He made some good friends down by the waterhole and learned to fight in a style that was effective, if not approved by the Marquis of Queensbury, but his academic training had to wait.

Jim therefore received a culture shock when, at the age of ten, his parents sent him to Sydney to boarding school, and he found himself amongst the gothic buildings, the quadrangles, and the sports fields of a pretentious establishment.

The mob of precious little bastards who shared his dormitory and classrooms were intolerant of his naivety and ignorance of things like football and cricket.

"Hey, Dopey," they taunted. "Where were you when Australia won the Ashes last year? Were you chasing a goanna up a tree with your black mates?"

They couldn't understand how anyone could be so stupid, and they couldn't imagine a world where communication was a scratchy radio while the batteries lasted and television was decades away. His fists ensured he was left alone, but they earned him few friends amongst his fellow students.

There always seemed to be something different about Jim. So, like Kipling's cat, he walked by his wild self until he left school and discovered the army and women. The army made him its own because he was tough and resourceful, and he earned the respect of his peers. The women loved him and were attracted to his latent strength and quiet gentleness. He looked at them under craggy eyebrows that matched his mane of sandy hair, which refused to yield to a comb or brush. He was a big man but stepped with the lightness of a fencer, and his legs already had a slight bow, born to fit a horse. Deborah, the girl in the car with him, was special, although there had been others before her. He didn't have to compete and didn't have to fight to maintain his position with women. They were more subtle.

He wouldn't fight for a while now. He lay in a brace with screws into his skull holding his head still, and his back screamed for relief as the pressure built into bed sores. The dope they fed to him through the drip in his arm helped, and he used all his charm on the red-headed nurse to get her to turn on the tap and give him a little more relief. He drifted into his memories again.

After the sickening thud of the vehicle crashing on top of their car, there had been an interval of complete soothing blackness, a nothingness that was neither night nor day, with the whole universe in suspension. A great soft blanket had been thrown over reality, blocking out everything including time and all feeling. It was the first awakening from that void that intrigued him and sent his mind racing, even now in the intervals before the pain took over again.

Like the memory of the crash, the scene was etched clearly in his mind, the picture razor-sharp. He lay on the road with Deborah's body beside him while paramedics fussed over them. He felt himself, a shadowy clone, rising out of the torn flesh that lay on the tarmac, seeing and hearing all from above but feeling nothing—a play being acted out before his eyes.

"We've lost the girl. Not really a girl—she could be forty, but she's a stunner. Look at that lovely auburn hair," said the driver of the ambulance. Road accidents were always a sad job.

"What about the bloke? He looks a hardy old critter, but that car bashed him about like he's been through a mincer. I'm trying to get a bit of saline solution into him, but he's just about gone too," replied the officer assisting him.

Jim became aware of Deborah's shadow beside him. Did he see it hovering there above their bloody carcasses, or was he aware of it with other senses? He remembered the smell, Deborah's smell, the delicious, tantalising scent that he associated with her love. It was there above the reek of petrol and hot tarmac. He felt a surge of freedom, of release. He felt Deborah hold out a wispy hand towards him as she drifted away. He tried to follow, but something held him back, drew him down into the twisted body on the road, and the image began to fade. It was all so quick, too real to be a dream, too strange to be real. The next awakening was in a hospital, and it was full of pain.

He'd loved Deborah. Theirs was a strange union consummated on infrequent and intense occasions when their careers allowed them time to enjoy a level of love and uninhibited sexual fulfilment granted to few people. As a member of the special response team of the SAS, his life expectancy was not great, particularly because he was the bomb disposal expert in the team. For her part, Deborah was a foreign correspondent for a large media group and seemed to end up in any conflict that was going. When the crash occurred, she was telling him about lying in a ditch in the Gaza strip and taking photographs as Israeli tanks shot over her head at stone-throwing Hamas youths. Each had lived for the moment and accepted the downside.

They'd often discussed death, talking it out until the fear evaporated in the passion of their love. They knew the end would come one day in the blinding flash of an exploding bomb or the slow agony of a bullet in the guts, but they never imagined it stalking them in a moment of tranquillity as they contemplated a week together—a week when they could forget hate and terror in the soft pleasure of their coupling.

The memory of Deborah drifting away from him after the accident, whether it was real or imagined, haunted him. He couldn't forget it, couldn't ignore it. He only had to close his eyes, and he saw it again, a tantalising glimpse of the great mystery of life—or was it? He was obsessed with the image, and it took over his thoughts, leading his imagination into corners he would have scoffed at before the crash. He told Sarah, the red-headed nurse, all about it in the wee hours of the morning as she sat by his bed trying to relieve the pain in his tortured body.

"Do you reckon there is a God up there?" he asked. "Do you reckon we have a soul that up and leaves us when we die? I can't for the life of me imagine what it's made of, but I sure felt as if mine was going to clear out after the accident, and I reckon I saw Deborah's go."

Sarah's nursing training hadn't covered that question, so she simply said, "I say my prayers every night like I was taught as a little girl. I hope someone's listening to them. You blokes can't expect to have all the answers. I'll get the priest in to have a yarn to you, if you like."

"No. If there is a God up there, I don't need one of those fancy-dressed clowns to talk for me," said Jim. "I get to feel pretty close to Him myself when I'm defusing a bomb. My relationship with God is personal. Deborah and I used to talk about some of the people we'd shared danger with—people who continually stick their necks out to help the vulnerable and the needy in the dark corners of the world. I listen to them but never can understand how it all works. Danger makes you more aware of life and the present, but the mystery remains."

"Tell me about it, if you like," suggested Sarah. She was becoming fond of the big strong man she had been sent to special. There was an inscrutability about him, a sense of the unknown. His horrific injuries were healing well, and she was aware of the latent power and superb fitness of the bronzed body she washed every morning. Most of his hair had been shaved off to locate the screws into his skull, but the clear blue eyes regarded her with a mischievous gleam when she let her guard down and his pain subsided for a while.

Jim told her how he had met Deborah in Iraq. She had been embedded in his unit as a war correspondent, accompanying them on patrols and armed with her camera, a notebook, and a curiosity that sought to look behind the obvious for the obscure motivations of the beleaguered people they were trying to help. She told him that she couldn't understand how the West could hope to win friends and influence the Iraqis by bombing the shit out of them, so she applauded the efforts of the Australian unit that was clearing the mines from the roads and trying to provide schools and medical help for the villages in the south of the country, as well as cleaning out the remnants of a militant cell. In her spare time, she visited the women of the village, forming strong bonds with some of them and understanding their motivations and needs.

Jim went ahead one day, down a gravel road, to defuse an explosive device they had identified near the bridge on the outskirts of the village. Once again he made that lonely journey forward on foot, his guts churning and fear tightening his muscles. He went through the familiar exercises, calming his body and focusing his concentration on the job in hand. He knew about the bombs and devices and understood their construction. He was quietly confident in his ability to disarm them, but he also knew that one day, he would strike a different one. There would be a trap he hadn't anticipated, and it would all end in a flash of heat and exploding metal.

He nearly bought it that day as Deborah watched from the troop carrier back along the track. He had quickly uncovered a corner of the device, and fortunately he recognised the end of a mobile telephone protruding from the package that was the bomb. He threw himself backwards and dived into a ditch on the other side of the road. Somewhere, in a house overlooking the site, an insurgent finished keying a number into his own phone, and the mine exploded, the blast carrying its cargo of nails and shrapnel over Jim's head as he pressed his face into the mud. Deborah was the first to get to him. That night, they planned to spend their next leave in Australia together.

"Why did you do it?" asked Sarah.

"I went to Iraq because I was sent," said Jim. "But now I look at the kids with one leg or hungry parentless faces, and I reckon I have to do something about it. Maybe I can make it a bit safer for them, but I wonder if we wouldn't have been better keeping our noses out of the mess in the first place."

It started him thinking about Deborah again. She had confided in him one day before a nasty assignment.

"I know about Islam," she had said. "I understand its virtues, and I know about the fanatics who corrupted it; I was married to one."

"How come you are a journalist out here with me?" Jim had replied.

"I escaped when he joined Isis," she had said. "He would have had me stoned if he had caught me. It turned me away from the restrictive aspects of Islam and the unforgiving rectitude of sharia law, but I still envy the certainty of salvation that so many believe, and I respect the code by which they live."

"I believe religion needs to be more than a moral code," Jim had replied. "Surely it is a relationship with the one you call God."

"I know," she had said. "I refuse to wear the burka, but I try to live by the moral codes of Christianity and Islam. For the rest, I'll just have to be satisfied with living a virtuous life and getting to know Him myself."

Jim dreamt about Deborah again that night. His body must have been recovering because the dream was vivid and realistic. Naked, they walked amongst the lychee trees on the remote orchard they had been going to visit when the accident happened. The sun had yet to rise above the horizon, but the air was balmy, and the dew settling on the grass was warm under their feet. They shared the ripe fruit off the trees as the kookaburras laughed in the forest beside the farm. They cracked the fruit between their teeth, the juice running down their chins and mingling with the dewdrops. They embraced, and her nipples grew hard as they penetrated the soft hairs on his chest. He rose to meet her, and they sank down into the welcoming grasses as the rising sun cast long shadows over them. He awoke to worry about how he could conceal the marks on the sheets from Sarah's amused eyes.

She had other things on her mind that morning as she quickly washed him and straightened the room.

"A journalist wants an interview with you," she said. "She told me you are to receive a bravery award in the New Year Honours List tomorrow, so they are sending round a camera crew. The doctor said they could come because he thinks you are up to dealing with them now. You've come a long way in the last two months. Don't forget to tell them about Deborah. She sounds quite a girl."

Jim welcomed the chance to talk to the press about the conflict in Iraq. It seemed so much more important than his own exploits, which he found too embarrassing to relate. He tried to explain the dilemma of the Iraqi people with their many sects and ethnic loyalties. He recounted how he and Deborah had studied both the Koran and the Bible, trying to find the common truth that explained the meaning of life and the nature of God and the hereafter. They found much in common in the religions and decided that most of the differences had their origin in the mass slaughter of the infidels during the Christian Crusades, as well as the bloody cruelty of militant Islam now. It seemed that the priests and mullahs interpreted the books to suit their own ends.

"Deborah and I concluded that if the conflict is ever going to be resolved, we need a better interpretation of the will of God (or Allah) and a better understanding of the nature of the human soul, always provided we have one," said Jim in his backcountry drawl.

It was all too deep for the young journalist, but she felt sorry for the broken man in the bed before her, searching for the truth that would explain the horrific experiences that led to his award. The fact that his current condition was brought about not by some clever enemy but by an ignorant hoon in a battered jalopy further excited her sympathy, so she encouraged his rambling while the camera crew took shots of the brace still screwed into his head.

"What about that fellow, Duncan MacDougal, in America way back in 1921? He claimed he had measured the weight of a soul at twenty-one grams," suggested the journalist with a grin. She had come across that piece of trivia only the other day.

"We both reckoned the protocols of the experiment were a bit unreliable." Jim smiled between the braces on his head while the monitor on the shelf above emitted a constant hum like a television set and scribbled green lines across its screen. "I often wonder why someone hasn't properly done the experiment," he added.

He lay back exhausted as the crew packed up to go.

The man in the next bed spoke up. He had not long arrived but was intrigued at the conversations he heard from behind the curtain that separated them, and he had listened intently to the interview with the journalist. "I heard all that rubbish you've been talking, trying to find out about the world through religion. You ought to have a look at what the scientists say about the universe. I've got the book by that brilliant physicist, Stephen Hawking, here. Have a read of that. Can't get over the fact that he did it all from a wheelchair."

Jim could sit up and read now, if Sarah reset his traction and adjusted his brace. There wasn't much else to do, so he started on the book, trying to understand and visualise the mind-blowing concepts of the start of the universe with the Big Bang and the collapse of matter into black holes under supergravity. Despite his lack of primary education, physics and mathematics had sparked his imagination at school, so he was not unprepared for some of the bizarre consequences forecast by Einstein's equations. He'd always been fascinated by the limitations set by the speed of light.

In the midst of his reading, the article about his award appeared on page four of the local newspaper, introduced by photos of his head brace and a delightful one of Deborah in her bikini as they frolicked on the beach at Mooloolaba.

"Wonder where they got that?" said Jim when Sarah showed him the pictures. "I would have been happier if they had left it out. She was married, and the Moslems get upset about that sort of thing."

He returned to his books, still driven by the recurring dreams of his near death. When he finished with Stephen Hawking, he sent Sarah out looking through the bookshops for more texts on the general theory of relativity and progressed to the physics of quantum mechanics. He found a whole world of very small things that hadn't been around when he was at school, and like most people, he had difficulty in visualising their behaviour. Many of the subatomic particles had been discovered or forecast since he'd left. He had put it all into the "too hard" basket and ignored the steady progress of humankind's knowledge of his universe. He read till he slept as the days merged into weeks.

Sarah helped him open and reply to the many letters congratulating him on his achievements and the sentiments contained in the newspaper article.

She handed one letter to him with a shaking hand. It came in a plain envelope and was unsigned. The message leapt off the page like the rocket-propelled grenades of the insurgents. Its message was stark and clear.

You have desecrated my wife and destroyed her body. The punishment for her adultery shall be visited on you. Live in fear.

He passed it on to hospital security and asked Sarah to vet the frequent visitors who now claimed to know the man in the head brace. He returned to his books, but the cold foreboding that had followed him down the road to many a concealed bomb came back to haunt his dreams.

He made a list of the subjects that intrigued him as he studied the new physics of the universe.

- What or who started the Big Bang?
- The laws of gravity say there must be a lot more matter in the universe than we can see or detect—black

matter and black energy. It can't be all made up of neutrinos left over from the Big Bang.

- There are four known forces of the universe. Gravity, electromagnetism, the strong atomic force, and the weak atomic force. Is there a fifth force controlled by thoughts?

- To fit his equations, Einstein postulated the existence of a cosmological constant that forces the universe to continue to expand in spite of gravity, which should make it slow down or collapse.

- Where is there room for God or the soul of man in all this?

Sarah came bustling in to tidy up the room again, and she frowned as she picked up the list. She was getting a bit tired of his obsession and the obscure concepts he kept telling her about. "Why don't you add the power of prayer? It will get you further than worrying about all that gobbledygook," she said, passing it to the man in the bed next door when he held his hand out for it.

"Can't mix up science and religion," said the universe man. "They don't mix. Besides, prayer is only thoughts expressed in words."

Jim knew he wouldn't solve the mystery of creation, and his ideas weren't all that brilliant, but perhaps physics could meet the spiritual one day. In the meantime, he needed something to hang on to, something to keep his mind away from the present. The prospect of life without Deborah and without the motivation of the SAS was like walking into an empty room. He would have nothing to guide him, no reason to face the difficulties of his rehabilitation. The memory of Deborah's death still haunted him.

He lay back in his bed and closed his eyes in thought, letting his imagination run and opening his mind to lateral ideas, just as they had in the tribal ceremonies he had attended with his aboriginal friends during corroborees at the bora ground on the hill above the station waterhole. Two words sprang into his consciousness: *thought* and *power*. He let them settle, turning each one over and fitting them into the complex ideas he had been reading about.

He remembered the list he had written down. What if thoughts existed on their own, had energy and mass, and could exert force? Gravity was conceptualised as acting through gravitons. Perhaps thoughts were the fifth basic force of the universe. Could there be *thoughtons* mixed up with all those neutrinos in the dark matter no one could detect? Did thoughts make up the cosmological constant that kept the universe expanding in spite of gravity? They wouldn't weigh all that much, but if E = MC², they'd pack a fair punch.

Jim needed a pee and pressed the buzzer for Sarah. When she had finished the embarrassing procedure of getting him to relieve himself into the bottle rather than the bed, he returned to his dreams.

Perhaps he was talking of God. Perhaps the soul of man was the sum of a lifetime's thoughts, or the pattern of *thoughtons* born in the maze of neurons as chemicals carried the spark of thought across the synapses. Perhaps, on death, they left to join the mass of other thoughts circulating in the cosmos, with good thoughts and bad thoughts cancelling each other out like protons and antiprotons. There would be so many more thoughts now than those that had coalesced to produce the Big Bang in the first place. Were they God's thoughts, or were the thoughts God? He recalled the biblical promise that the righteous should sit with the

Lord. Maybe their thoughts contributed to the spiritual power of the universe.

Jim smiled for the first time in days. It was all a bit over the top. He told Sarah, laughing at himself but intrigued with the idea in spite of its improbability.

Sarah simply shrugged her shoulders. "You've lost me, but if it makes you happy and you can forget about the pain for a while, I am all for it," she said.

He had enough to think about for a lifetime, fitting all the pieces together like a jigsaw. He felt it didn't really interfere with his personal relationship with his maker. There was still room for the relationship between God and humanity. For some reason, he remembered the threatening letter he had received. He shivered as a wave of fear brought goosebumps to his limbs.

He awoke the next day to see a dark man in the flowing white robes of an Arab striding through the ward towards him. Terror swept over him. Adrenalin flooded through his veins as it had in combat, but this time flight and fight were both impossible. He was confined by the brace on his head and the traction on his legs, stretched out and secured like a dummy for the executioner. Jim frantically squeezed the nurse call button and shouted to the other occupants of the ward who were similarly confined. He felt his bowels let go as the knife descended, and he tried to ward off the blow to his heart.

Sarah rushed into the ward in response to the terrified yells from its inhabitants and the frantic jangling of the alarm bells. Screaming for help, she threw herself on the back of the man bending over the bed, where her patient lay feebly trying to fend off the blows raining down on him. She clawed at the stranger's face and clung to the arm that rose and fell, thrusting the bloody knife into the helpless form beneath him. The attacker swatted her off his back as he might rid himself of a fly and walked to the door muttering, "Allah Akbar." The hospital security guards apprehended him as he reached the corridor, but it was too late for Jim Dougherty.

Sarah wept over the coffin of her patient and tried in vain to follow the funeral service through her tears. She had come to love the big man who had faced death so often and tried to clinically analyse its implications. She would pray for his soul and ask God to make up for the injustice of his passing.

As she left the church, she looked up at the boundless blue of the sky and smiled as the kookaburras started laughing again. If thoughts were really as powerful as he imagined, he and Deborah would make some big waves up there in the cosmos. She hoped they would get together.

A RELUCTANT JOCKEY

The main street was not formed, just a wide space with the railway property on the south and some town buildings on the north, and generally littered with discarded petrol tins, which provided a venue for car obstacle races when country visitors to town were feeling somewhat merry. Later, I remember this area being the site for at least one race meeting for station hacks. In at least one of these I took part, but I did not gain a place because my riding abilities were somewhat below standard, having arrived at Julia Creek with very little country experience.

—Notes written by Jack Heussler

Jack leapt from his horse in triumph and slammed the yard gate shut behind the little herd of weaners. Perhaps that would shut up some of those smart alecs who teased him about his horsemanship at every opportunity. He reckoned he did a pretty good job getting those youngsters in all by himself—not that he wouldn't be pleased to get back to building the yards out at the five mile. Jack was good with an adze and a fair mechanic by 1920s standards, and he earned his jackaroo's wage in those areas even if he was a bit new to the stock work.

Away in town all afternoon, his boss, old Harry O'Grady, came into dinner with a grin like one of those fossil dinosaurs down where the creek washed against the base of the sandy rise.

"Hear you did a good job with those steers today, Jack. I've got news for you. We decided to hold a race meeting," he announced. "Bloody town's got to 'ave a race meeting if it's going to be called a town. Reckon we'll run the horses up the main drag. Start west of town on Cloncurry Road and finish up just past the pub. Everyone will get a good look at the finish that way. Told the committee that you'd ride old Lightning."

"Hang on a minute," Jack said, bristling. Previous confrontations with the big bay gelding had usually ended with him on the ground a mile away from where he should have been. "Never ridden in a race in my life, and neither has Lightning. I'll never hold him once he sees all those flags, and he'll spook at the noise."

"You can both learn together," said Harry. "If you can point him in the right direction, he'll win hands down. You might have a bit of trouble pulling him up after, though. I reckon if you ride him the fourteen miles into town in the morning, he'll be settled down enough to race in the arvo. You can mount him in the yards here, and we'll go ahead in the car and open the gates for you. Let him cool off a bit in the railway yards. We've got nothing else that would do any good."

It was far too much notice for an event like this. Fear and consternation grew in his belly like a cancer as the weeks went by, and the teasing by the other jackaroos increased in intensity. "Remember where the winning post is. You've got to go past that," they jeered.

Early on the appointed day, Jack's shaking knees took him down to the yards at Min Min Downs. Harry held

Lightning by the bridle and one ear while his jackaroo mounted and screwed down in the saddle. He opened the gate and jumped clear before running to start the old Model T. He'd be lucky to beat the horse to the first gate by the way he departed. Three miles down the road, Jack managed to bring his steed down to a canter in some semblance of control, marvelling that he was still aboard.

Jack sneaked into the railway yards the back way. Constructed to hold cattle awaiting transport on the railway, the yards fed a loop line just south of the town. Clouds of thick dust, stirred up by the animals milling round in the pens, regularly drifted over the little settlement to the annoyance of the residents. Today, the horses contributed to the chaos as the yards were used for stables and saddling paddock combined. The south-easterly wind lifted more dust. It eddied round people, horses, and vehicles, traversing the improvised race track up the main street.

Multicoloured flags and bunting flapped and flew from every vantage point, and even the old cars parked along the footpath were cleaned and decorated. Ladies in their finery and cloth hats laughed round the tables placed outside Mrs. Horton's Tea Rooms. Attended by their suited partners quaffing beer purchased at the pub farther up the street, they consumed their share of the heady stuff mixed in with Mrs. Horton's offerings. Moist drink glasses left muddy rings on the dusty tables, somewhat spoiling efforts to create the atmosphere of a Paris brasserie.

Busy officials in all sorts of garb hurried to execute the important things that officials execute. The street was closed to traffic, and all the empty petrol tins, usually scattered over the area between the town buildings and the station, had been removed and used as markers to define the race track. The deep footpad, worn by the Chinese gardeners carting water for their vegetable plot across the road from the tap fed by the railway water tank, had been filled in. (It was just as well because some revellers had broken the spring of their Whippet Tourer on it, doing obstacle races through the tins the previous Saturday night.) A winning post was erected at the corner of Mathew Street, just past Emerson's Hotel. Hoping to attract custom from both directions, the bookmakers from Cloncurry and Hughenden set up their stands under colourful umbrellas on the footpath between the pub and the tea rooms.

When Jack went across to find a bite of lunch, Harry issued him with a bright red silk shirt and introduced him to the steward, a big man who had knocked round many a racetrack in the bush. As the chief official, he exhorted Jack to ride clean and fair. Jack's only worry was getting to the other end of the course.

Jack eventually found himself at the starting line with Lightning, stimulated by all the strange sights and sounds and up on his toes again after his short spell. Drawn on the inside, Jack had the greatest difficulty keeping his mount behind the line and pointing more or less in the right direction.

"Go!" yelled the starter as he dropped his hand holding the white pillowcase.

Lightning started out with the rest, but the professional jockey next to him had an idea the big gelding might be able to go a bit if he had a good run, so he slashed him across the face with his riding whip as they started the race.

"Get back there, ya big bastard," he snarled.

Never having been treated like that before, Lightning shied two paces sideways, kicking over a petrol tin and nearly wiping out a bystander. Jack lost a stirrup and was halfway out of the saddle before another bystander hit the horse on the rump with his hat and neatly dodged the retaliatory hooves. Fortunately, the resultant sudden change of direction brought the horse under Jack again, and he was able to concentrate on surviving the ensuing pig roots as Lightning humped his back in the belief that the elimination of his rider might ease his torment.

"Gallop, ya bugger, gallop!" yelled someone over the laughter as he threw a tin at the reluctant steed.

Lightning took off after the cloud of dust stirred up by the hooves of the vanishing field. Jack, thankful he had insisted on the big knee pad saddle rather than the jockey pad offered back at the yards, frantically secured the errant stirrup. "Look at 'im go!" he heard as Lightning started to reduce the impossible margin and passed Harris's Garage. There, the town dogs, caught napping and sniffing wheels when the main field went past, were now ready and alert. They seized their opportunity and came at him from all angles, further increasing the speed and erratic direction of the bolting horse.

Lightning flashed through the finish line to the cheers of the crowd with Jack hanging on for dear life and the baying pack at his heels. It took him a mile to slow down the frightened animal, and when he eventually regained control, they returned to the railway yards the back way. "Bad luck," said Harry. "He galloped all right when you got him going."

Jack furiously went in search of the steward. "Did you see what that bastard did to me?" he demanded.

The steward threw back his schooner and smiled. "Heard you had a bit of trouble," he said. "We talked to the bookies and decided not to take any action. Seems no one bet on you anyway."

It took a fair few beers and one or two kisses from the local flappers at the ball that night before he calmed down, but by the time he rode a somewhat chastened Lightning home the next morning, he could see the funny side even if the horse couldn't.

CONFUSION

People. Bloody people everywhere. I sat, beer in hand, watching them circulate in the big hotel lobby. People! Then why was it so damned lonely? I was happy by myself on a hundred thousand acres out west of the 'Curry. Here, there were a thousand people an acre, and I was lonely. Not that I didn't enjoy watching them. I did. I kept thinking what they would look like in their fancy clothes out in a cattle yard with a few scrubbers chasing them.

I felt sorry for that poor bugger over there with two kids out of control and his little painted missus tearing strips off him about something. Then there were those sheilas coming through the revolving door. Those bodies and those dresses, and you got a good peek at what was hanging out in front. Bit young for me, though, and they looked a little sour. And look at that. Wouldn't I like to be sitting here waiting for her? Her tailored skirt and pretty soft blouse matched her flowing brown hair. Probably in her forties, medium height with lovely long legs. Her perfect figure was momentarily framed in the glass doorway. But her face reminded me of something vaguely familiar. The whole lobby brightened as she smiled at the doorman and set a course that would take her past my table. I pretended not to look.

She caught my eye as she came closer. Her face lit up, and she smiled. Was it at me? Or was it someone behind me? I damned near looked back to see, but that would have been rude. Besides, it just might be me. Panic! What to do? Aw, to hell with it. Why not? I smiled back.

"Hi, John. What brings you to town?" she enquired brightly as she hove to in front of my table.

Bloody hell! She does know me. I scrambled to my feet, table and chair bouncing off my legs in my haste. Thank heavens I saved my drink from spilling down the front of that beautiful skirt. Better answer the question.

"Just down for a conference. I'm representing the local shire," I stammered. She must be from out of town too. I might get a clue if I ask her. "What about you? I didn't expect to see you here," I said lamely. I had nearly fallen over scrambling to get her a chair.

"Oh, I am the token woman on a board, and we meet here once a month," she replied.

That didn't help much, but it was great talking to her, so I might as well try for a bit more. "Have you got time to sit down and have a drink with me?" I invited with my fingers crossed. I had now secured the chair.

"Sure. We have finished our meeting, and I am footloose and fancy-free. I did so enjoy the last drink I had with you. I'd love a gin and tonic, but you probably remember."

Of course I didn't remember, but I thought she had a twinkle in her eye as she added the last bit. I went to get the drink. Where the hell had I had been talking to this dream woman? I was hopeless at remembering people. I could remember a cow I had seen in a mob a year ago, but people were impossible. Still, one would think I would remember her—unless it was a con. Perish the thought. I had heard that it happens down here. Beautiful women seduce old hayseeds from the bush and relieve them of their wallets. Perhaps in the electronic age, they might get a man's bank account. I'd better be careful. Never could remember the passwords anyhow, so they were safe. But she looked too nice for that. Where on earth could I have met her? Should I come clean and ask her? No ... bit late for that.

"What do you do with your spare time when you are not being a token woman on a board?" I asked while delivering the gin and tonic. I thought that was cunning and should give me a clue.

"I still do a lot of consultancy, so that, and a failed marriage with two kids, doesn't leave me a lot of spare time," she replied. "But I do like the garden, and I try to do a bit of writing."

The writing bit interested me. "Tell me about it," I said. It was getting me nowhere, but we had a fascinating discussion on creative writing for the next half hour. I was getting hooked. She was delightful.

That was when I saw Wot's'name bearing down on us. He had been at the conference from somewhere to the east, I think. I remembered his pink shirt. Bloody boor he was too. How do you introduce two people when you don't know either of their names? "You two know each other?" I asked.

"Yes, of course I know Jane. She planned all our aged care facilities." He looked at Jane and smothered her with a smile that told her to ignore my stupidity.

It all came flooding back. She and I had spent a magic two hours in Mount Isa Airport waiting for a plane in the Club Lounge. An expert on nursing home design, she had been helping to establish a facility in one of the nearby towns. I had been interested in that, and she had enjoyed a few of my yarns about the Gulf Country. Wow, what a relief!

But now Wot's'name was all over her like a rash. If I didn't bust into that conversation soon, I'd lose her anyhow. Wish I could remember his name. If I knew where he came from, I could change the subject. "You going back to the conference, boss?" I asked.

"No," he said. "But don't go away. I've got to go the men's room. Then I'll buy you a grog."

I had to move fast. "I can't lose you for another two years like I did in Mount Isa," I ventured to Jane. "Let's escape tonight, and I'll take you to a great place I know for dinner." I put the emphasis on Mount Isa to let her know I remembered. Tricky.

"Yes, I'd like that," she replied with a conspiratorial smile. "I have a few things to do. Why don't you come to my room at six thirty, and we can go from there when I have finished? The number is …"

"Can I get you something?" interrupted the waiter. Then Wot's'name returned. Crikey, he was quick. It's always the same. You never have time to think in the city.

We had another two rounds, and then Jane insisted on shouting. I still couldn't remember his name or what town he represented. Anyway, he did most of the talking, so Jane and I simply nodded; I didn't have to exercise much ingenuity. Jane made her excuses and rose to go. She dropped her room key beside my chair. Smart thinking, that! But it was 699, or was it 669? Which way up was the damned thing. I bent over to look. Wot's'name knocked his umbrella over as he leant over me to see. Jane grabbed her key and departed in a line to the lifts as straight as the seams in her stocking. Bugger! 699 or 669? I didn't have a clue. I left Wot's'name after a few minutes to go to my room and sort out the numbers. At least I knew her name now.

I got out of the lift. She was sitting waiting for me. "I don't trust your memory," she said. "The room is 669, his name is Dave, and he comes from Emerald. By the way, it's three years since that afternoon in Mount Isa. And don't you dare forget that you are taking me to dinner tonight. I want to hear more about the Gulf Country." I wrote it all down just in case. One gets confused in the city.

RISING WATERS

Sam was on a nostalgia mission—or was he just laying ghosts? While travelling in the general area for business, he had been tempted to detour up the little valley where he had spent his early childhood. *Best confront those thirty-five-year-old memories before I embark on a marriage I have been subconsciously avoiding for years,* he thought. After leaving the car by the roadside, he walked down the grassy slope, keeping an eye on some adjacent steers. Yes, the rotting stumps of his parents' old shack were still there beside the creek, as was the big fig tree with an old piece of sawn timber still nailed across its branches. He sat on the remains of the back landing and remembered. He was a boy again …

The cubby had perched on those limbs overlooking the garden. Large enough to sleep two small boys, it could shelter eight-year-old Sam and his friend Jason, snug in their sleeping bags, whatever the weather. The corrugated iron roof had been extended to cover a small porch in front of the opening. The cubby served as a pirates' lookout as well as protecting the interior. A rope ladder could be pulled up to keep out any stray girls— not that there were many kids of either sex living along the country lane that meandered beside the water course. Sam's real home had squatted close beside the large waterhole in the creek not far from the tree. The house was painted a dirty brown all over, and Sam reckoned it looked like a giant cane toad about to jump into the pool. Sam's Dad told their friends, Jim and Julie Dawson, how he caught a fish for breakfast off the back veranda.

"Just walked out in my pyjamas and threw out the line," he explained.

"You didn't have any 'jamas," claimed his wife Mary, and the grown-ups laughed.

Grown-ups laugh at strange things.

"Wish I'd been there," quipped Julie.

"That would have been fishy," observed Jim, and they all sniggered again.

"Must be something we're missing," Jason whispered in Sam's ear.

The Dawsons were frequent visitors and had moved into their home on the high ground across the road the year before, so they didn't have far to walk over for an evening's festivities at Sam's place. He noticed that, besides the visits becoming more frequent, the number of bottles to be carried up to the bin next morning also increased. The boys had discussed the outings and how their parents enjoyed getting together. They welcomed the development because it always raised the possibility of Jason sleeping over in Sam's room. Besides, sleeping over often led to a fishing trip next day.

"Come on, you two," Sam's dad would say. "We'll take the boat up to the dam and get some real fish for dinner. Bet I can catch the biggest one. The wall is only a couple of miles up the creek."

The boys treasured the time with Sam's dad. They built the tree house together, and he showed them lots of funny little animals and plants that could be found on long walks in the bush. Pity that Jim Dawson always seemed too busy to come with them, but sometimes he let them listen to the footy on the radio with him; he knew about all the players.

Julie came fishing with them one day. It was a bit of a disaster, really. Sam's dad spent the whole time baiting her hook and showing her the most elementary dos and don'ts of fishing. It was funny how girls simply couldn't understand the important things in life. The grown-ups both enjoyed the expedition; Sam could tell by the way they looked at each other. When they got home, Mary had started on the wine again, and Jim hadn't recovered from the night before. Sam and Jason retreated to the tree house, but they heard voices raised in the living room.

"Wot the bloody hell were you two doing, sneaking off with the kids?" asked Jim. "Hope you weren't feeling her up in front of them. I thought the swapsies were supposed to stop at breakfast time."

"Don't be crude," Julie quietly implored. "Look at the fish we caught. But I think we all ought to be a bit more careful when the boys are around. Don't know what they would have thought if they had seen you cuddling Mary in the corner last night."

"You can't talk. You were having a good smooch after the lights went out—if that's all you were doing," accused Mary. "Anyway, I don't give a stuff. Seems we are all bits of swingers."

"Cool down, Mary," cautioned Sam's dad. "You do get a bit reckless when you have a few under your tail. If these Saturday nights are going to turn into orgies, we ought to bed the young fellers down in the tree house. They will be safe enough there, and it will be a real treat for them. At least they will be a little way from the action"

Sam and Jason didn't hear the details but knew there was some confusion about who was cuddling whom. They decided that when they grew up, they would be pirates and wouldn't have any women around. Not that they minded Julie. She was nice when she wasn't fishing, and she sneaked them special cakes if she was cooking. She didn't complain about everything like Sam's mum. When they found out they were to sleep in the tree house, they reckoned it was the ant's pants. All night to themselves without the grown-ups interfering in anything! They would be able to pretend all sorts of things and could suit themselves when they went to sleep.

It didn't happen for a month, but one hot Saturday, the Dawsons came over for a late afternoon swim in the water hole. Sam and Jason got out the old tractor tube and defied all boarders. There was much splashing and ducking and laughing, and everyone had a great time. Jason and Sam agreed that they hadn't seen their parents having so much fun together for ages.

"Why don't we barbeque that steak we got yesterday?" suggested Mary.

Out came the beer and the wine while Julie went home to make a salad. Under instruction, Sam and Jason found some wood and lit a fire in the old barbie. Sam's dad dealt with the steak and onions, and Jim found he had to help Mary in the kitchen. Sam told Jason that it was the best feed he had had since he started listening to the Argonauts—that would be a year ago now. To cap it all, they found some have-a-hearts in the fridge after the washing up.

"Can we take them up to the tree house and eat them there?" asked the boys, eager to begin their adventure. The possibility of sleeping out had already been mooted.

"It might be a bloody good idea," observed Sam's dad. Mary was already into the gin and tonic.

Equipping the expedition was not unlike sending Scott to the Antarctic. Sleeping bags, a torch, and their special blankets (Jason's from across the road). An Esky had to be filled with the have-a-hearts, cold raspberry drink, and some water. The boys couldn't understand what the water might be for with all that raspberry drink. Then they needed their shanghais and a couple of toy guns to repel the invading hordes that were likely to attempt to storm the castle. They could change into pyjamas up there after all the fighting and feasting, but teeth had to be cleaned before departure.

Julie helped Sam's dad hoist all the gear up to the cubby. The special blankets were her idea, as was the somewhat embarrassing goodnight kiss. Music had started exploding from the house, so Jim and Mary were obviously well advanced with the evening's entertainment. After having deposited the boys, Sam's dad escorted Julie back to the house. He didn't think the boys would notice him take her hand as they walked.

"I kinda like your mum," whispered Sam, watching them.

"Yes, I think your dad likes her too," agreed Jason. "I wish my dad was more like yours. He's always going crook at Mum these days. Mum says he is just angry because he lost his job."

"He doesn't look too angry when my mum is around," commented Sam. "I wish she wouldn't drink so much of that gin stuff. It makes her act silly, and I know Dad doesn't like it. She rouses on all of us when she's had some."

"I wonder what grown-ups do when they have a party?" Sam didn't have the answer. It was hard to understand how everyone could be friendly and having fun when the boys went to bed, and the next day they were at each other like a mob of roosters.

"Why don't we sneak down and have a look later on?" suggested Sam. "Let's get the torch and see if there is anything we can hit with our shanghais while we are waiting." The searchlight beam sprang from the fortress, and missiles frightened the daylights out of a stray cat that was sitting on the fence and minding its own business. Next, the rose bushes took a pounding. Eventually, after running out of ammunition, they decided to investigate the mysterious world of grown-ups.

They sat for a while and tried to pick out the constellations Sam's dad had pointed out to them on previous evenings, but half the sky was obscured by a bank of clouds, and the odd flashes of lightning in it revealed a blue wall of rain coming down the valley.

"We best go down and see what they are doing before it starts to rain," suggested Jason.

The descent from the fig tree and the approach to the living room window was conducted with commando precision. They were able to lie down and watch with complete safety through the bottom panes. They clung together, eyes wide with surprise, curiosity, and horror in quick succession. These were their parents, and the whole thing threatened their stability in a way they could not understand.

Sam's dad was getting Julie a drink from the side table. He came back, sat beside her on the couch, and received a kiss for his trouble. They sat close together, talking with their bodies touching, and the boys saw him put a protective arm round her shoulders. The radiogram had ceased playing the loud jazz music that Sam and Jason had heard from the cubby. Now the volume was muted, and the soft strains flowed sensuously through the window above their heads.

"I thought the music was for dancing," observed Jason, but Sam pointed to the other side of the partition.

Through the dim lights, they could just see Jim and a very unsteady Mary, passionately kissing and swaying to the rhythm of the music.

"Her blouse is all unbuttoned," whispered Jason.

"Yes, but look what she's doing to him," breathed Sam as she slid down the zip of his fly, and his trousers dropped around his ankles.

"So that is what swapping means," said Jason when Jim slid his hands under Mary's skirt, and she sank back against the edge of the table, pulling him towards her.

The first big drops of rain hit the boys, and they scurried back to the shelter of the cubby as the lights came on in the house and thunder announced the full fury of the storm. They didn't hear the expletive that followed, but they did see the commotion at the front door.

"I must run back and shut up the house," yelled Julie over the noise of the downpour.

"I'll come with you and see you home," volunteered Sam's dad.

"You'd better both bloody stay there till morning," shouted Jim.

Mary giggled.

"What about the boys?" asked Julie, concern in her voice.

"They are better off asleep in the cubby than with us," retorted Sam's dad. "They will be quite dry there and as safe as anywhere. We'll rescue them first thing in the morning. I might as well stay over at your place till then, by the looks of the situation here."

The boys got into their dry pyjamas, snuggled into their sleeping bags, and wondered about what they had seen.

"Think people do the same sort of thing as my dog Mick?" They both pondered the question. It was a bit difficult to discuss it with the drum of rain on the roof, and the sound soon put them to sleep anyhow.

The deluge poured down hour after hour until the early morning light struggled through to reveal a sodden landscape. Neither the boys nor Jim and Mary were awake to see it, but the other parents sat in the house across the road greeting the misty dawn with a guilty kiss and concern about the boys. The local run-off was already swelling the creek.

Jason thrashed around in his sleeping bag, but Sam, all curled up in the blankets, shivered with fright. He was dreaming.

His mother, Mary, partially dressed in a white robe, ran round and round a small room, pursued by a fierce dog. Sam was perched on a table near the casement, frozen with fright. He knew he should open the window and jump out, but he couldn't move. Mary laughed and shook big, oversized breasts at the animal, which seemed to infuriate it all the more. Sam sweated and crouched low on the table, hiding his eyes when the mastiff's great jaws caught her dress and ripped it off as she ran. The house shook, and the table fell over in the confusion, Sam went with it. The dream shattered.

Years later, the locals still argued whether they felt an earth tremor or whether the collapse of the earthen wall of the dam up the creek had shaken the countryside. Abnormal rain after a long dry spell was the agreed cause of the catastrophe in the paper the following day. Whatever the reason, the roar of the approaching torrent roused the boys and released their nightmares. Startled, they rushed to the porch of the tree house and watched as the waters in the billabong beside the house came alive. They bulged and splashed and shook. They heaved upwards in a great irresistible surge. They filled the banks and splattered outwards like some giant cow pat dropping from above. A second wave advanced down the valley, sweeping the debris before it and bearing everything up onto its crest. Fence posts and dunny cans, motor cars and toy carts—the rubbish and the treasures of the valley were born aloft on the surging brown maelstrom like a giant carpet sweeper clearing all before it.

Sam and Jason, spellbound, clung to the railing of their porch as the flood lifted the dirty brown house off its foundations, and like the giant toad they had imagined, it set off down the creek. They caught a glimpse through the mist of Jim, naked and desperate, helping a screaming Mary out of a window before it all disappeared in the murk.

The water surged round the tree. The flotsam caught in the lower branches and threatened to topple it, but the roots had spent decades burrowing into the soil, and somehow they held. The cubby sagged and bobbed dangerously close to the torrent, and the boys clung to the porch in fear.

They were still clinging there, wide-eyed, when Sam's dad and Julie waded through the receding flood to rescue them.

Sam reached down and picked a flower from the old garden. He cast it into the water in memory of Jim and

Mary, his mother. Now it was done. He remembered all the love and support he and Jason had received from Julie and his father. Marriage could work. The rising waters had forced new beginnings, but old memories would last.

LONELY

She sat down on the same bench as me. It was the far end of the bench of course, but she sat down! Wouldn't have expected that. A nicely dressed young woman— beautiful too, I think. Wish I could see more clearly. The colours seem to fade nowadays, but I liked the way she carried herself as she walked. She'd come down the path from the ferry terminal on the river near the hospital.

Good watching people who come over from the city to visit inmates in the wards. *Residents*, the staff have to call us now. Bloody silly, that. Everyone knows we can't leave the damned place even if we want to. We're here for good. Glad I talked them into bringing me out in the chair and leaving me on the bench a while. They know I'm harmless and can't get away. Fall flat on me blooming face if I try to stand up. At least I know the river is over there, and the city is piled up behind it, even if I can't make out the buildings. I like the smell of grass and trees. Yes, and I can smell that bloody smoky diesel in the boat. Injectors need cleaning. Can't see too well, can't hear too well, but I sure can smell.

Reckon I can smell the girl too. Pretty smell, like the scent of flowers we had in the garden as a kid. I can remember that. I can remember the garden running down to the waterhole, an oasis in the wide dusty plains. I remember the smell of dust in the westerly wind too, and the cool, clean smell of wet ground after rain. Wish to hell I could remember yesterday. Can't even tell you what I had for dinner. Not that there's much to remember in here. Same old routine. Get you up in the morning, change the nappy and clean up, get into the chair and down to breakfast, then sit in the room and think. Always remember the nappy change. Funny—I don't mind the girls doing it as much as the men. Reckon that's the end when someone has to wipe your bum. Don't know how I got to this state. I remember what it was like before the war, though, at those tennis parties in the bush, and the barbecue afterwards, and the girls in short dresses. Gee, but they were good times.

The bench is shaking. She's got her head in her hands and is sobbing her heart out. The bunch of flowers has fallen onto the dirt. Maybe that's what I smelt. I'd pick them up, but I'd wind up down there with them. Never get up again.

Now, there's another smell—sweaty, fear, animal scents. She's young and vulnerable. Time stands still when they're young. Fear, sorrow, hope, joy, love— emotions take over and consume the kids till something else happens. I should do something for her. Lend her a handkerchief, perhaps? No. Mine's all snotty.

Wonder what's the matter? Probably hankering after some old geezer inside. Be better going up and giving him a hug than snivelling out here. Funny, that: as soon as you get old, no one wants to touch you, let alone hug you. Probably the smell of piss, which never seems to leave you. Gee, but I'd like her to visit me and give me a pat. So long since anyone has given me a pat. Probably wouldn't remember them if they did, but it would be nice at the time. Think I would remember that.

I shuffle up the bench towards her. She glances up and inches away. The waterworks open up again. Best

I look at the river. Never can be any bloody use when you get old. "Can't be that bad," I try. She looks away, snivelling. I shuffle back to the end of the bench.

Don't like the look of that lout coming out of the hospital ... Bloody hell, he knows her. She smiles through her tears.

"I thought you'd ditched both of us. You haven't forgotten your mum's birthday?" she asked, picking up the flowers.

"Didn't wait for you. I took up the clean clothes. Silly old fart wouldn't know you anyway. Let's go to the pub." He reaches for her arm.

She throws the flowers at him and flounces off. I kinda like that girl.

THE ORCHARD

Pride of ownership gave way to terror that first night at our new macadamia orchard. Sharing my love for the bush, my husband, Richard, and I had spent the afternoon scrambling through the encircling forest looking for burls and logs, which he could fashion into unique pieces of furniture for our new home. I kept an eye out for ferns and plants to adorn the garden that I had already started to plan.

Richard's woodworking skills would also be applied to renovating the dilapidated little house under the fig tree. My heart sank every time I thought of that kitchen with its missing drawers, sagging doors, and rotting bench top. I looked with horror at the floor covered in torn linoleum, but I soon recovered as I gazed out the broken window at the view over the mountain valleys to the sea. Tendrils of mist rose above the waterfall, and the shifting light continuously changed the colours of the forest clothing the slopes below me. I knew the prospect would give me constant pleasure, and to the west, there was nothing dilapidated about the neat rows of macadamias waiting to be tended and loved. Shed and house could be rebuilt, but the bush and the orchard would live and grow.

We decided to camp the night and absorb the essence of the place, bare though it was, until our possessions arrived. Besides, Richard's mother wanted to inspect the new acquisition the next day, and we both wished to present it favourably. She hadn't approved of me when he'd brought me home, and she still couldn't accept that her daughter-in-law had dark skin. A picnic under the fig tree might take her mind off the house, but years of accumulated grime would be hard to disguise in the time available. Nothing could conceal the shabbiness of the buildings.

We cleared a space in a large, bare room for our mattress to the sound of approaching thunder. The storm came down on us with the evening shadows. Lightning struck so close that it fizzed before the thunder, and wind howled through the cracks, carrying driving rain with it. The ceiling spewed water in cascades. The sudden darkness as the power went out left us feeling for a dry spot on our mattress. There would be no water for toilets or kitchen until power was restored days later.

The storm passed, soon to be replaced by footsteps on the roof and a slithering noise. "Is it in the ceiling or in the room with us?" I asked Richard, shuddering. He couldn't hear above the groaning and creaking of the big clump of bamboo outside the window, which conjured up all sorts of intruders in my imagination. We clung together on the wet mattress until the dawn released us from our fears.

We padded out onto the veranda and warmed out bodies in the rising sun, secure in our privacy and in the love this new adventure would cultivate. The mountain air was rejuvenated after rain, and the clear, crisp view from our veranda lifted our spirits even as we observed that the roof of the shed had narrowly missed falling on our car.

"The valley is so beautiful. I think I could enjoy it whatever the discomforts if it wasn't for your mother's visit," I said with a sigh. "There is nowhere for her to go for a piddle, the water has turned to mud on the floors, and how can I possibly make an interesting picnic without water or power? She'll never let us forget it."

"Don't fret, Jules." Richard was his soothing best. "We'll try to put her off. If she insists, she will have to make do like the rest of us."

The pictures of Richard's mum making do set me quivering like one of her jellies.

But I'm usually a practical sort, so we cleaned up the floor as best we could and set off for the city to buy a ready-made picnic and collect our guest if it proved inescapable. We slid and spun our way up the driveway, and I closed my eyes to the precipice on my side of the road.

"Bugger," said Richard.

A great branch lay across the road, sprouting dense foliage. We stripped down to our underwear and descended into the mud with the axe and saw from the toolbox we had brought to the farm. An hour later, we had the road cleared at the cost of muddied and scratched bodies. We scraped them clean and dressed over the top. Surely Richard's mum would let us shower at her club, but we were late already and feared our reception would be cool.

A peek along the veranda of the club as we arrived confirmed her state of general agitation.

"Steward," we heard, her voice imperious.

"Yes, Mrs. Sinclair," said a frock-coated waiter complete with tray and napkin.

"A tea strainer, if you please. You have not brought me a tea strainer."

"Oho …" My knees were getting that jelly syndrome again. "Please, Richard," I begged. "Please let's not take her out to the mess back at the orchard."

"She'll get over it."

"There you are, Richard," came his mother's voice, full of authority. "What on earth kept you? You look like you crawled through the hedge."

Why did I feel so ignored? How could I possibly ask for a shower and a change of undies? It was OK for

Richard, but every little incident reinforced my sense of incompetence and ate away at my self-esteem. Richard never saw my black skin, but others did, and they had a thousand ways of putting me down. My own family took it as an attack on their pride that I had married a white man.

I took Richard's arm as we walked up the steps. Richard and I would make it in the natural beauty of the orchard as long as the older generation got the hell out of the way. In the meantime, Richard was telling her not to come because there was nowhere to piddle.

"So you've bought a heap of rubbish," she said. "There must be something good about it. You'd better take me out to see it."

Richard put his arm around my shoulders, and I took courage from his support. After all, she was his mother, and I loved him so much.

"We can take you out there and show you the view and the orchard," I said. "But you will have to imagine what we can make of the rest. Richard can work wonders, and I will help him as much as I can, Mrs. Sinclair."

"Oh, don't be so formal," she replied, to my amazement. "You know my name is Anne."

"If you really want to come out, you are welcome," said Richard, "but we know it is a mess now, and we don't need to be told."

"You never did like being corrected, Richard."

"We thought you might enjoy a picnic under the fig tree, Anne," I hastened to add as I squeezed Richard's arm to calm him down. "We will have to visit the shops in town because the storm has made it impossible to present anything nice at home."

"Then you had better clean yourselves up a bit. I'll get the waiter to show you the bathrooms," she said.

We cleaned ourselves up as best we could and then departed to do our shopping, so the time had advanced to 11:00 before we could get back to the club to pick her up. Richard talked about the macadamia industry on the way up to the orchard, enthusing on the prospects of a new industry of some worth being developed in Australia, so it was lunchtime before we arrived at the dilapidated shed and began to prepare our picnic.

I went into the house only to be confronted by a black snake in a somewhat aggressive mood. I quickly grasped a wooden broom left there during our cleaning efforts in the morning and attempted to defend myself and dispose of the reptile. Hitting it with the broom seemed ineffectual, and the best I could do was press the broom down on its neck while it struggled to escape. I yelled to Richard to bring an axe.

Not Richard, but Anne appeared at the door, axe in hand, and she cut off the head of the struggling snake. I dropped the broom and leant back against the bench, shaking all over and trying to catch my breath. Anne wasn't much better, but she came over and gave me a hug.

"You'll do for a daughter-in-law," she said.

"You'll do for a mother-in-law," I said. "I'll need help to plan a kitchen."

DANCING MEMORIES

Through a red haze of pain, his mind struggled for consciousness. A leg lay twisted awkwardly over a tree root, and his head throbbed with each pulse of blood to his injured brain. Sensation crept back into his body, wet from the overnight dew in the ditch beside the gravel road. A passing car had thrown stones over him as he lay under a bush on the edge of the forest, his red checked shirt concealed by the long grass and roadside vegetation.

After struggling into a more comfortable position, he tried to remember, tried to think. *What happened to me? Where am I?* The more difficult questions like *Who am I?* and *Where did I come from?* had not yet penetrated the mists that swirled round inside his mind. The answers were concealed behind an opaque wall, gossamer thin and fragile yet impenetrable. He could not go back further than the rush of tyres that had wakened him and the wet grass that concealed him.

He crawled up the steep bank to the roadside, holding his chest as pain seared through his body. He looked around and staggered down the track, ignoring the laughter of the kookaburras and the attacks from an irate magpie as he passed beneath its nest. The forest rose on either side of him, green and forbidding, and the white gravel of the roadway led him on, led him forward, a painful path to nowhere. So many cars passed, so many drivers fearful of dealing with a druggie or bum. Bent over to nurse his cracked ribs, with his clothes muddy and frayed, he lurched from gutter to crown on the uneven surface. His physical strength was well disguised by his stooped gait, and his vacant expression had an addict's glassy stare. It wasn't until a kind old couple came past that he got a lift. He gratefully sank into the soft upholstery of their back seat until they deposited him at the emergency section of the hospital in a little town inland from the bustle of a coastal city.

The mists blanketed his mind again as the staff asked his name, whether he had a Medicare card or driver's license, and what happened to him. They found no wallet or money, but there was a credit card in his shirt pocket in the name of Joe Davidson. Joe Davidson—he had a name now but got no further. Who the hell was Joe Davidson?

The staff in admissions weren't interested in someone without a Medicare card, and they were full anyhow with more urgent cases, but they couldn't throw him out. Somehow they found space in a back ward. After obtaining a medical opinion that prescribed rest for his amnesia and the blow to his head, the nurses cleaned him up and put him to bed, strapping his chest to support his injured ribs. They informed the police and put an advertisement in the local rag asking if anyone knew a Joe Davidson.

His body healed quickly, and the sisters remarked on the development of his limbs and the fitness of his superb physique. His memory returned more slowly, lost in the confusion of relearning the world. They called in a psychologist to assess his condition.

"You must remember something," said the doctor. "A blow to the head seldom results in more than temporary loss of memory, and even then it is usually selective. Tell me what you can remember about your early days."

"Oh, I remember growing up as a small boy," Joe recalled. "I remember the heat and the flies in the corrugated iron shack we called home. It was out on the Mulligan River Channels, built beside a great sand hill. I used to toboggan down the sand from the lip of the dune on an old piece of ply wood. Dad tried to get me interested in the cattle, but I wasn't meant to be bush kid. I kept all the old copies of *The Illustrated London News* under my bed. They were the only window to that other world I knew existed. I spent any spare time I could find listening to music on the old gramophone we kept on a bench beside the dining table. Dad used to storm into the house calling me a lazy nincompoop and telling me to get outside and do something useful.

"It sounds as if it was a pretty rough life," observed the doctor.

"Yes, it was. But the desert had its good times too. I remember sneaking away on my own when I couldn't play the gramophone, fishing for yellow-belly in the waterholes or walking along the sand hills at sunset." Joe smiled as he remembered the magic sunsets in the dry air of the west and the millions of stars that shine on the dunes every night. "I don't think I was ever a cockie's son at heart. I heard the music in my ears all the time, and sometimes it was the music of the desert, but it had nothing to do with the drudgery of our lives, scratching a living from the dry land.

"Like so many others out there, Mum and Dad thought they were establishing a great cattle station that they could hand on to their children," he added. "They had plans for a grand homestead, fenced paddocks, and satellite cattle yards up and down the river. Every cent they earned went back into the property. Next year was always going to be the season that would get them out of debt, but in the end, they couldn't even find enough money to send me to boarding school."

"You're going well," said the psychologist, trying to reassure him. "Try to keep thinking of the old days. They tell me your ribs are healing, so there is no need to keep you here. I'll recommend you for discharge in a couple of days. You'll eventually achieve full recall, I think." He rose and left Joe in his bed with what memories he could find.

What was he going to do when they released him? The question was too hard, so he lay back in the pillows and thought of his childhood. He relived again the long days mustering cattle, the breakfast in the dark, and the ride out in the first rosy light of dawn. That part was pleasant enough with the cool of the morning wafting across the flood plain on the small breezes and the abundant bird life of the channels greeting the new day with enthusiasm. But later, the white heat of the sun reflected off the bare clay pans into his face and dried the sweat from his back before it could wet the thin fabric of his shirt. As the miles passed, the little pony had to jog to keep up with the big horses when they crossed endless dry watercourses under the coolabahs only to be confronted by another expanse of baked earth. After they had the cattle in hand, the animals had to be chased from the shade of the trees in the creeks and persuaded to face the dry, hot track to the station yards.

He remembered the dinner camps when they rested themselves and the stock beside a waterhole. The hot, dark tea brewed in a quart pot burnt his tongue, and the little bush flies swarmed onto his corned beef sandwich or crawled in his eyes. Then there was the long ride home, his bum raw from the jogging pony and his head throbbing from the migraine while his lips stuck together from thirst.

"This is a man's country," his father would say. "You'd better get used to it. It will be yours one day. Now, get into that backyard and push a few cattle up to the pound while I draft them. Mind that cocky horned mickey, though. He'll flatten you if you turn your back on him."

His mind returned to the present. The hospital bed was comfortable. Its soft whiteness closed around him, insulating him from his memories and dulling his pain. He would have to leave it soon. He would have to start life again. He couldn't remember what brought him to this pass, but he had the feeling he was running away from something. Fear lurked in the background. He had dreamed of running away from his childhood. He had lain in that other bed on the Mulligan, waiting to grow up so he could flee the country, so he could leave behind him the discomforts and dangers and cruel discipline of the desert, so that he could start another life. He gave up trying to remember and slept.

But the nurses had been told to keep him talking, to keep dredging up memories of his past.

"How did you go to school? Do you remember anything of your school days?" asked Sarah, the young sister, as she ended her shift and elected to sit with him for a few minutes. They had all grown fond of the big, strong young fellow in the back ward who was struggling to reconstruct his life. "You'll have to speed up the memory thing when you leave here."

He looked at the soft oval face framed in its curtain of brown hair now released from her nurse's cap, and he noted the concern in her hazel eyes. Another face swam into focus. It was the motherly face of his Aunt Mavis, who had come for a visit to the station one Christmas. Yes, he remembered her now—his father's sister who lived in Sydney. She talked of leafy suburbs and shops and bright clothes and music, always the music. She had given him the cuddles his mother never had time to deliver and his father never thought about. She had told him wonderful stories of life in the city and the boats that sailed across the harbour. But more fascinating still, she told him of the ballet and the dancing. She told of flying across the stage, of spinning on the tips of her toes until she was giddy, and of soaring aloft on the arms of her partner in a series of graceful lifts.

"It is gradually coming back to me," he assured Sarah. "You reminded me of my Aunt Mavis. She was the one who rescued me. I hid in the bathroom while she had a furious argument with my parents and offered to take over my education. If they couldn't afford to send me to boarding school, I could live with her in Sydney and attend the local state school. She would teach me to dance and play the piano in her living room. I remember her pleading with my father, and I think she was lonely too. She relished the prospect of sharing her music with a member of her family."

"I can't see an old bushman liking that idea too much," observed Sarah, breaking off as two bearded louts in motorcycle leathers entered the ward closely followed by the wardsman.

"You blokes get to hell out of here," hissed the man in hospital fatigues, stepping in front of them. "It's way past visiting time, and there are sick people trying to sleep."

"Heard you had a Joe Davidson here," said the big fellow with the tattoos.

"He don't want to see no one and can't remember a bloody thing anyhow. Now, get off with you." The wardsman shepherded them out the door.

"Be a lot healthier for him if he don't remember too much," muttered one of them as he left the ward.

Sarah looked back at her patient and found him curled up under the covers, shivering with fear.

"Sorry, nurse," he muttered, struggling to sit up and regain his composure. "I still can't remember what happened before I got here, but whenever I get close to it, I have a dreadful sense of fear, disillusionment, and flight. I always seem to be running away. I ran away from home and the desert so long ago, and I ran away to the love and security of Aunt Mavis. But there is something else that is more recent and more powerful, something crueller and more urgent. Those two brought terror into the ward, a terrible feeling of panic. Please make sure they can't get to me. Can you make a note that I'm to have no visitors?"

"You'll have to face your demons one day," said Sarah, but she left a note at the nurse's station and the front desk before she went home to worry about her strange patient.

The police came next day. "There's no Joe Davidson on the missing persons lists," they assured him. "You'll have to remember a bit more before we can help you. We'll do some more research but haven't much hope of finding who did this to you. In the meantime, you'd better start remembering—and don't leave town without telling us." They rose to go leaving Joe floundering in the mists of his amnesia. He was due to face the outside world this morning and had nowhere to go.

He confided in Sarah when she visited him before starting her shift mid-morning. Together, they found a cheap boarding house listed in the telephone directory, and he noted the address as Sarah took him down to the administration section to check out. The credit card was accepted, but Joe cringed as he signed the four-figure receipt. How long would the card last, and what would he do if he ran out of cash before he could establish his identity and his skills?

The boarding house lay in a garden of weeds situated in a gully on the edge of town. Its unpainted rooms were peopled by the unemployed, the junkies, and the hopeless. It was presided over by a sleazy woman who saw opportunity for profit in a credit card held by a man in a red checked shirt living in some place remote from reality. He could sign his name now, Joe Davidson, in a similar scrawl to that on the back of the plastic. It was similar enough for the landlady but not quite the same as the confident flourish of the specimen signature.

He watched television and wondered where he could have fitted into the strife-torn lives depicted on the screen. He read the newspapers, marvelling that he was regaining some of his life skills in spite of his forgotten memories. He kept to himself, nursing his aching head back to health. The landlady fed him, grossly overcharging him for her services via the credit card … until the payments stopped.

"Get yourself into the bleeding bank and sort it out," she snarled. "Can't stay here if ya has no money."

After stumbling through the glass doors of the bank, he presented his card to the woman behind the front counter under the financial logo.

"My name is Joe Davidson," he said. "I've lost my memory, and it appears there are no funds left in this account. I'd like to know if you hold other accounts in my name."

"Can't discuss your details without identification," she stated. "What's your password?"

"I don't know," he said. "I can't remember a damned thing."

"Sorry, I really can't help there. Privacy laws say I can't tell you anything until you're identified. Do you remember your date of birth?" she asked.

"I don't know," he repeated.

"I can see your difficulty," she observed. "Here, try signing your name on this form, and I'll talk to the manager."

She watched frowning as he slowly inscribed *Joe Davidson,* attempting an awkward flourish at the end like the original.

"I'm afraid it's not good enough," she pronounced, deciding that it was probably stolen. "I'll have to keep the card. Please come back when you have the necessary identification. You'll need eighty points."

He didn't tell her that the police had come to the same conclusion.

Dick Ramsay stood tall and strong next in the queue, watching as Joe pleaded in vain for help, his blond head sinking onto his hands and his shoulders shaking inside the red checked shirt.

"Please don't take that from me," he implored her. "It is the only thing that tells me who I am."

"Best go to the police again. They're two blocks down on the left. We really can't do anything about it here," she replied, her stern face softening at his misery.

Dick stepped forward and put a firm hand on his shoulder. "Here, come on, Joe, or whatever your name is.

I'll buy you a coffee down the street. If the bloody bank can't do better than that, they don't need my account either."

Two big mugs of coffee and a plate of lasagne later, Dick had the full story, or as much of it as Joe could remember.

"You sure got a problem," Dick remarked. "First thing is to get you out of that hovel down on Creek Street. They aren't your type down there. There's a good place the other side of town, and I can get you enough money for the first week's rent there. Have to pay it back one day, mind you. Then you'll need a job."

"They tell me I can't work without a tax file number," Joe said with a sigh. "And I don't know what I can do anyhow."

"You ought to know how to wash up," said Dick. "I hear that big RSL Club on the coast needs a kitchen hand. There's a bus that runs over there every day. It only takes half an hour, and I'll help you sort out the paper work for the job."

Joe clung to Dick's back as the big motorbike took them round the town and over to the coastal city, where they sorted out accommodation and a job washing dishes.

Apart from Sarah's interest back at the hospital, friendship and support had fled with his memory and whatever caused its loss, so Joe reacted with gratitude and trust to the assistance and companionship offered by the young man in the motorcycle leathers. He soon found his confidence returning, and with it his ability to relate to those around him. *Best kitchen hand the club has had in years* was the general opinion round the stainless-steel benches behind the serving counter at the RSL. He started doing odd jobs out in the dining room.

That was how he came to be in front of the big auditorium at the end of a meal when they ran a track from a recent production of *Swan Lake*. He looked up into the eyes of the prima ballerina, larger than life on the silver screen, as the music flowed through his veins. He looked further back to the dancer in ballet tights gracefully displaying his movements. His legs came alive, wanting to spin and leap with the shadows moving above him, an operation rendered more difficult by the armful of dirty dishes he carried. The mists cleared swiftly, and his mind fled back to his old life in the ballet.

He froze as the memories surged into the vacant spaces of his mind connecting all the disparate pieces he had dredged up since waking up beside the road. He remembered the joy of dance overshadowed by the pain of the constant training, the endless extension of muscles and joints beyond the limits of endurance. But recollections of his small success on the boards soon gave way to a more powerful emotion, one that started in his loins, pumping adrenalin until his chest hurt. He felt again his love for the ballerina, for the feel of her, for the look of her, for the joy of her smile and her soft words. He felt again the rapture of his expectations and the promise of their fulfilment.

Then he experienced the crushing blow of her rejection, of his replacement even before he had tasted her love. Fearing disruption to the harmony of the group, the producer had dismissed him, delivering the final devastating blow to his dreams.

The insincerity of the world he had worked so hard to enter had overwhelmed him and destroyed his energy, his ambition, and his career. He remembered now the kind, strong faces of the bush people, but he couldn't go back, couldn't face the realities of the desert, couldn't face the family he had scorned.

Painfully, he took the dirty dishes back to the kitchen, his tears falling into the scalding water as he washed. He remembered leaving Sydney. He remembered driving north and picking up the two young fellows who had asked him for a lift at the petrol station. The blow to the back of his head had come out of the blue as they stopped by the roadside to relieve themselves. It was a blank after that. He rang Dick as soon as he returned to his flat.

"You'd best tell me the whole story," suggested Dick after he arrived on his motorbike in response to Joe's urgent summons. "How did you get into the ballet in the first place?"

"Just as some people are born with a love of nature, I was born with a love of music and dance. I loved the stories behind the productions. I loved the rhythm and the melody. I loved the expression and the movement of dance. Aunt Mavis nourished them all. She gave me a dream to chase. She inspired in me a passion for the ballet and a determination to succeed," answered Joe. "I became completely immersed in it, to the extent that annoyed and frustrated my father, who hoped I would show some interest in the cattle or the property during my visits home for school holidays. I remember him complaining to my mother that I was turning into a bloody pansy and would never be any good in the bush. They knew their sacrifices would be in vain and that there would be no one to inherit the station when they were gone."

"Must have been a bit bloody lonely," suggested Dick.

"I worked too hard to be lonely. I fell asleep at night with my muscles screaming from their over-extension and my joints painful from their dislocation. But I was good, and I got better with Aunt Mavis there to encourage me and rub Dencorub into my aching limbs. She drove me unmercifully when I faltered. She built my confidence and finally secured me my place in the ballet company." Joe's eyes fell to the floor in shame as he remembered his aunt.

"She put so much love and effort into my career, and I threw it all away over my stupid infatuation," he confessed. "I know that now. I worked it out as I fled north in my little car with no destination in mind, but I didn't think of that as I caught that beautiful body in my arms in the dance."

"She must have had some feelings for you," suggested Dick.

"No, she was using me to get at the ballet master," said Joe. "They were all using each other. Just as bad as the two louts I gave a lift to on my way north. They only wanted my car and my money. I still worry about them."

"No need to," said Dick. "We had a yarn to them at the bikie club. We told them you wouldn't remember them as long as they didn't step out of line again. It's cheaper that way than sending them to prison. So are you going back to the ballet?"

"No. I reckon if they'll have me, I'll stay with the club. Might get to handle the music when they know more about me, and I might even try and open up a ballet school in my spare time," said Joe. "I've run away from love, and I've run away from Aunt Mavis. Before that, I ran away from the desert. Can't run away forever, and I can't go back. I couldn't face the old man, and I'm not running away again."

"Don't knock running away," counselled Dick. "I've been trying to do it for years. I call it change. It's where you arrive in the end that counts."

MY RED NOTEBOOK

A crow carked as it landed on the dead branch outside my study window. I leant back in my chair, removed my glasses, and let my mind wander from the task in hand. I had been sweating over the report on the new orchard for the Smith family. The day was oppressive with thunderheads building in the west, and I was hungry. Never did get around to cooking myself a decent feed since Hilda left. I wondered how she was handling that retired radiologist she had run off with.

Poor Hilda. I still missed her even though the place was oh so much more peaceful without her constant criticism. I heard again her voice berating me. "Reg Western, time you fixed that tap in the kitchen, and the front lawn needs mowing. Don't know why I married a bloody academic."

Life had been better in the beginning, but we were never really suited, and I always resented the need to become a bureaucrat in the state government department rather than letting my mind fly in the CSIRO research division where I had started. Hilda had refused to move from her family in Brisbane, so we had raised our kids there, and I had spent a lifetime advising farmers in the Lockyer Valley on whether to spray or fertilise.

I made myself another cup of coffee and picked up my red notebook. No need to hide it now that Hilda was gone. I leafed through the tattered pages, putting off going back to the Smith family orchard. The red notebook was my escape mechanism. In it, I recorded my frustrations and my desires, my fantasies and my hopes. I even recorded my few escapes from the chilling sameness of the job and the prison that my marriage had become. There were some high spots. The outbreak of Hendra virus that I had helped to diagnose in some horses had been exciting. I'd written a lot about that. And, Fiona …

The telephone's shrill summons startled me out of my reverie. The dark panelled wall of my study swam back into focus, and the shelves full of books displaying pictures of dissected animals or ladders of DNA on their covers brought me back to the reality of my life. The photo of Fiona fell out as I put down the red notebook.

The voice that vibrated out of the earpiece held a touch of panic. "Jim McAlpine here," it said. "Want you to come straight over. That mob of young ewes we bought look like they're stepping on hot coals. They're walking around with their heads in the air. Looks like five or six are down already." I hastily replaced Fiona's image, ignoring the touch of guilt I felt whenever I saw it.

"Reckon you could come out and see what's wrong with them?" Jim continued. "I'll meet you at the station at two o'clock."

Damn, I thought. He should be able to work it out himself, but I knew he could ill afford to lose too many stock. At least I could take the train to save driving through the traffic, and I could work on the Smiths' orchard design on the way. I swept the papers off my desk into the big briefcase that always stood beside the door and headed for the rail platform across the road from my house.

I did some more daydreaming on the train as we clacked over the joints and left the town behind. Orchards that I had trudged over looking for insects and fields that I had sampled for fertility slid past my window. The scent of macadamia blossom couldn't get into the sterile air conditioning of the train, but I imagined it all the same. It brought back my sense of longing for more meaning in my life, for someone to share the intimate details of the day, for someone to communicate with, to talk to, to feel contact with, and even—dare I say it—make love to.

I thought again of Fiona and the photograph I had replaced in the red book. I saw the girl with the dusty backpack and tatty shorts whom I'd met in the pub at Birdsville and who had pleaded to go with me on my field trip. I was looking for a weed that had reportedly been introduced by the afghan camel drivers last century, and any company on those lonely sand hills would be welcome. She wanted to see what was over the Mulligan because she hadn't been there, and she hadn't seen the desert soften under the stars after the sun went down and the heat of the day drifted upwards. Why not? It seemed a valid excuse.

As so often before, I relived those five days we had spent marooned by the unseasonal floods in the middle of what should have been a desert. <u>We had d</u>ays and nights as the warm rain came down, cocooned in our own little canvas world without the possibility of interruption and soaring ever higher on a passion that ebbed and flowed as it was consummated. We pushed our guilt to one side. The red-brown waters of the Mulligan slid past our tent, insulating us from that other world of responsibility, of loyalty, of fear. Even then, we knew it must end. Her free spirit would know no bounds, and I was hemmed in with my job and my responsibilities to my growing family. Neither had sought an extension of our bliss, so when the little boat came over the flood to get us, we stepped aboard knowing that our paths, so entwined for five days, would diverge as steeply as they had come together. I left with her image in my pocket and started my little red book.

The train rattled over the points at a siding. *Silly old bugger,* I told myself. *You're becoming maudlin in your old age.* I started again on the Smiths' orchard.

Then we arrived. Jim and a young woman were sitting in their car opposite the station as I joined the crowd spilling across the road. A Mack truck, its load looming gaunt and towering through the dust, sounded its horn amidst the squeal of its brakes. Startled, I spun round, knocking my briefcase against the knees of the old man behind me. The lid flew open, spilling papers that were whipped away by the wind. Little tubes of soil samples rolled across the gravel while syringes of numerous shapes and sizes speared the road like a druggie's hideaway. Jim and his blonde niece, later identified as Robin, helped me gather up the mess while the Mack truck roared past, suffocating us with a blanket of diesel fumes and road dust.

Robin ran down the footpath, stamping her foot on my errant papers and running to catch the next, with the wind tugging at her hair and my neatly drawn charts scrunched in her hand. I repacked my briefcase in the back of the car, flattening out the sheets as best I could. I retrieved my little red book that had spilled onto the street along with the plans for the orchard. One has to have something to confide in, so the little red book was privy to a number of embarrassing secrets that I wouldn't like lying about on the road. I checked for Fiona's photograph. It wasn't in its usual place behind the back cover. I frantically searched the area again, explaining my concern rather inadequately to Jim and Robin. We couldn't find it, so perhaps it was still back in my study.

Jim brought me back to the job and his worries. We walked through the paddock and looked at his sheep. Several were dead already, and the rest were wandering about like high-stepping ballerinas. I'd never seen it before in the east, but page 1,024 of the reference book flashed up in my mind's eye. I was good at visualising things; it helped my research in those distant days when I was going to conquer the world of science. "Annual rye grass toxicity," I diagnosed. "But you've got no ryegrass. Not much grass of any kind with the drought on."

"I got a bit of rye grass hay from South Australia," said Jim.

"Take them off the hay, and those that aren't dead should recover," I advised as I headed back to the car. I was lucky to pick that, but ARGT, as it was called, had always fascinated me. The fact that a certain worm would crawl up a particular species of grass with special bacteria on its back and select a special spot on the seed to build its nest was hard to conceive. That the special bacteria should secrete a special poison for a hungry sheep to eat was indicative of precise planning on the part of Mother Nature. It would have been nice to spend my life in research sorting it all out, as I had hoped to do in my young days.

We shifted the sheep, and Jim drove me back to the station, telling Robin at every opportunity how brilliant I was. It wouldn't do my reputation any harm, but he could have gotten it out of a book himself if he'd known where to look.

When I got home, I searched for Fiona's photograph in vain. I felt the light had gone out in my secret room. It was the one thing that connected me to that other life, the one I dreamed about where I was a professor of genetics who went and did wild things with his mistress. I had missed the turning all those years ago when I'd let Fiona go. I'd missed the chance to be different and soar into the unknown, born aloft by a love we both shared. I had secreted her photo in my red book through a difficult marriage and a dull career. Now, it too was gone, leaving me floundering in nothingness.

The next day, Robin arrived. The gravel scattered amongst my rose bushes as she burst into my driveway, the hood down in her red sports car—the same red as the cover of my little red book.

"I found your photo," she cried, waving it from the front seat. "It looks like the woman I work with up north." She bounded out and squeezed past me into the house. "We take tourists white-water rafting on the Tully River. It gets really exciting when the floods push us along a bit."

I took her into my study and told her a little of my week with Fiona and how I had kept her photograph hidden for so long.

"I'm driving up north today. Why don't you come with me?" she suggested, her eyes twinkling with mischief and her face alive with enthusiasm. "Fiona would love to see you. Time you went down some wild rivers." A magpie warbled his agreement from the branch beyond the window.

The adrenalin surged through my veins. I was being offered a second chance to escape from the sameness, the routine, and the expectations of the bureaucracy. I could find release from the loneliness of my kitchen.

"I've got a departmental committee on genetic services tomorrow," I groaned.

"They'll have to do without you when you're dead. I'll help you pack," said Robin, heading for my bedroom and the battered suitcase on the wardrobe.

I did it. I rushed out of my house and slammed the door, with my bag in my hand and my little red book under my arm. I stood a foot taller as I tossed my luggage in the back seat and settled in beside her.

As we sped up the road in that little red car past rivers and fields, with the wind of our passage ruffling my beard, I took out my little red book and sketched the girl beside me as she sang to the wind. But the face that appeared on the page, with the blonde hair streaming behind and the lips smiling for fun, was the face I had cherished so long in the photo.

CHARLIE'S STOCK ROUTE

The most noticeable thing about Charlie was the two inches of grey-looking woollen underpants that used to hang out over his trouser tops. That, and his lined and weather-beaten old face. The little boy used to stare at him and wonder how he ever got a razor to follow the mounds and valleys. More discerning people like the boy's mother didn't notice the wrinkles because of a big, wide, and infectious grin.

Charlie was a boundary rider whose job it was to mend the fences and look after the flocks for his employer. He also had responsibility to see that the drovers and sundry bagmen who travelled the adjacent stock route didn't convert any of the fat sheep on his side of the fence to mutton. Or perhaps cut the fence and graze their hungry animals on the better pastures under Charlie's control.

However, the most important thing to know about Charlie was that he was a communist—a real, live, card-carrying communist at the time of the Great Depression in the 1930s. He had books on communism, all in red covers. He had a radio set that occupied most of one wall of his tiny tin hut. It was one of the early short-wave sets, and each amplification stage had to be tuned separately to the accompaniment of a great many squeals and whistles. But it could receive Radio Moscow. It gave Charlie constant reassurance that the revolution would come soon. He also had a little kelpie sheepdog, which he called Revo, in anticipation of the time when he would be in charge of a chain gang with all the district's capitalists tied together building roads.

The capitalists were the station managers and selectors whose holdings bordered the stock route. Down that strip of land came many drovers with their large herds of lean Territory bullocks destined to be fattened on the flooded plains of the Channel Country. Or there were big flocks of sheep looking for grass and going for the sake of going. They all made camp opposite Charlie's hut, where they swapped a yarn. Or perhaps two lame horses for one good one spelled in Charlie's horse paddock. Charlie made a good business out of that, and the little boy heard the adults say it sounded like capitalism. The bagmen too had heard of Charlie's communism and camped at his hut expecting him to share a killer with a fellow member of the proletariat.

This created a monumental problem for Charlie. On the one hand, as a communist, he could not ignore the plea for the redistribution of wealth contained in the request, but on the other hand, he was loyal to his employer and would not countenance theft. He solved it in a novel way.

When they finished shearing, the station managers would put all the stray sheep into a yard and invite the neighbours over to claim their animals. Charlie came too, and there were always sheep from farther afield, dropped from travelling mobs. Cost prohibited their return even if the owners could be identified. Charlie would say, "Yair, they look like mine boss," so he and Revo would depart with his little flock, which would be fattened up in his horse paddock for the bagmen.

Some of the adults applauded this. They had differing opinions about Charlie, but all were agreed that communism was a wicked thing and that some undefined "they" should stop it. The idea of a chain gang was ridiculous and the concept was abhorrent. The little boy was somewhat confused about communism and capitalism and thought that a kind word and a hug were probably better than either of them.

The discussions always got round to speculation as to how Charlie had arrived at his current situation. Some said that in his youth, he had started out in business but had been caught embezzling funds. The ensuing sojourn in jail had warped his mind. and he had escaped to the bush on his release. The little boy knew this was not right because Charlie always returned the marbles he lent him.

Another theory was that he had once been married to a rich lady who had deserted him for a gentleman with grand ideas and an inherited fortune. Charlie had opted for the celibate life of a boundary rider and was determined to despise women and anyone with money. The little boy disagreed because he has seen him chatting to his mother. Not that she had much money, but she was a girl.

No! The little boy thought it was all too complicated. Charlie was probably just a poor old man who had grown up in the bush with not many opportunities and was too shy to take those that did come to him. He wondered whether Charlie had ever had the chance to enjoy "tuppence worth of dark" at the pictures with a pretty girl like the big boys described in lurid detail.

He understood why Charlie might want to change things. After all, the tin hut would be hot, and the bunk looked uncomfortable. His monthly supplies of tea, sugar, flour, tobacco matches, and rations were even less than they had as a family, and they were much less than the manager of the big station who wore a dinner suit to tea each night. Yes! It was clear that Charlie might want to make a difference.

What nobody understood, least of all Charlie, was that he had made a difference. The drovers went on their way with a fresh horse and a tale to tell at the next campfire. The bagmen went down the road with a spring in their steps, food in their bellies, and corned meat in their tucker bags. Perhaps a bit of kindness and forethought is better than any of the *-isms*, mused the little boy.

The End